"You haven't heard my proposal. It's actually quite honorable."

Aurora pushed her plate away unfinished and looked heavenward. "Okay, hit me with it. Then I'll tell you exactly what I think of it."

"I'll return one of your diaries to you," Luke told her, "for each date you have with me. Incidentally, I only intend to keep the last five diaries, so our agreement would extend for five dates. After that who knows?"

"And if I don't agree to this?"

Luke shrugged. "I guess I'll get to know you through your diaries."

Some of our bestselling authors are Australian!

Emma Darcy...
Helen Bianchin...
Miranda Lee...
Lindsay Armstrong...

Look out for their novels about the
Wonder of Down Under—
Where spirited women win the hearts of
Australia's most eligible men.

Watch for more thrilling romances
with rugged Australian heroes
in 2002!

Lindsay Armstrong

A QUESTION OF MARRIAGE

THE AUSTRALIANS

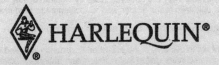

HARLEQUIN®

TORONTO • NEW YORK • LONDON
AMSTERDAM • PARIS • SYDNEY • HAMBURG
STOCKHOLM • ATHENS • TOKYO • MILAN • MADRID
PRAGUE • WARSAW • BUDAPEST • AUCKLAND

ISBN 0-373-12208-X

A QUESTION OF MARRIAGE

First North American Publication 2001.

Copyright © 2001 by Lindsay Armstrong.

Visit us at www.eHarlequin.com

Printed in U.S.A.

CHAPTER ONE

'FOR crying out loud, Luke,' Jack Barnard said *sotto-voce* as he eyed the retreating, ramrod-straight back of one of the most militant women he'd ever met, 'why the hell do you put up with that…that gorgon? Getting anywhere near you is like trying to break into Fort Knox!'

Luke Kirwan grinned and picked up the list of messages his secretary had just presented him with before departing indoors. 'Miss Hillier?' he drawled. 'Believe me, Jack, she's invaluable for keeping…' he paused '…students of the female persuasion at bay.'

Jack Barnard stopped looking irritable behind his spectacles and laughed aloud. 'Don't tell me they still make a nuisance of themselves? It's not a problem I would have a problem with, by the way. Herds of sweet young things panting to be in one's bed. Mind you—' he looked reflective '—with the delectable Leonie Murdoch in one's life, perhaps not. Is that what this is all about?' He gestured comprehensively to include the house behind them and the garden around them.

Luke Kirwan rubbed his blue-shadowed jaw and squinted up at the home he had only recently moved into. It was a two-storeyed, attractive, hacienda-style home perched on Manly Hill, a bay-side suburb of Brisbane. From the terrace, where he sat enjoying a beer with his long-time friend Jack Barnard, who was also his solicitor, they had sweeping views out over Moreton Bay towards North Stradbroke Island. 'Maybe,' he said pensively and shrugged. 'Maybe not. I was looking for an investment when it came on the market, then I thought it might be nice to live here.'

Jack Barnard regarded his friend quizzically. It was hard

to imagine a more unlikely professor of physics—and one of the youngest to gain his chair at the university he taught at. Because Luke Kirwan was about as far removed in looks from the proverbial absent-minded professor as one could get. Tall, lean and dark with a hint of rapier-like strength, he also possessed a pair of brooding dark eyes that made him look arrogant even when he wasn't—although there was no doubt he could be arrogant.

Add to this a boundless energy, a fine intellect and the capacity to look through people who bored him with complete indifference—and you had the kind of man women found electrifying, Jack Barnard mused ruefully. He himself, he went on to think also ruefully, was much more the archetypal professor. He was short-sighted and supremely absent-minded.

But it was on his mind as he surveyed Luke Kirwan that a worm of discontent might be niggling away at his friend. One would have thought that, by now, Luke and Leonie Murdoch might have tied the knot—they were a spectacular couple and had been together for a few years. In fact he, Jack, had been quite sure it was about to happen when he'd first heard about the new house. Now, though, he wasn't at all sure of it.

'May I point out that you spend very little time at home, Luke, so this could all be quite wasted on you?' he said, and added delicately, 'Have you and Leonie fallen out in any way?'

Luke Kirwan gazed expressionlessly out over island-studded Moreton Bay as it danced and glittered beneath a clear blue sky. Then he transferred that enigmatic dark gaze to his friend and said with a quizzical little smile playing on his lips, 'Jack, what will be, will be.'

'In other words, mind my own business?' Jack hazarded wryly.

'In *one* word, exactly.'

*   *   *

A week later, Aurora Templeton set her teeth and commanded herself to stop shaking.

True, she was breaking into someone's house at the dead of night, but only to remove something that rightfully belonged to her. So it wasn't stealing. It wasn't really breaking and entering because she had no intention of breaking anything, as for entering—yes, well, that could be a moot point, she conceded as she shaded the torch with her gloved fingers. But if you couldn't retrieve your property by any other means, what else were you supposed to do?

She'd also thought this out thoroughly over the past week, she reminded herself, and now was no time to get the wobblies.

But the fact was, it was more nerve-racking than she'd anticipated. Despite having lived, not that long ago and for a long time, in this solid, two-storeyed, hacienda-style house set in its lovely garden—which was how she came to have a key and the knowledge that an easement ran behind the house leading to another street—it was impossible not to feel intimidated by the consequences of being caught in the act of what some might consider robbery.

It was also a heavily overcast night, humid and very still but poised eerily, one couldn't help feeling, for a good storm.

All the more reason to get it over and done with, she told herself briskly, and inserted the key into the deadlock of the laundry door. It opened smoothly and noiselessly. Not that there was anyone home, she'd made sure of that.

The new owner was interstate and she knew that no new burglar alarms, locks or vicious dogs had been installed. Indeed, without a key to the deadlocks, the house was virtually impregnable—all the windows had decorative but effective wrought-iron Spanish grills to protect them, all the doors were thick, solid, hardwood timber.

She slipped silently through the laundry and kitchen into the hall without the aid of her torch after allowing her eyes to adjust to the darkness, and had to smile faintly at how her teenage years came back to her. The laundry door had been her favourite means of entry when arriving home after her curfew had expired.

But she put the torch on, although veiled again by her fingers, for one swift glance around the hall in case the new owner had laid his furniture out differently, to see that there was still the same clear path to the bottom of the stairs. Then she froze and flicked it off at a slight sound. Just a tiny knock really, but it was difficult to establish its source.

And she waited motionless for a few minutes, in her black jeans and polo-neck sweater, with her heart beating uncomfortably.

How she didn't scream as something furry wrapped itself around her legs, she never knew, but the large cat then sat down beside her, purring quietly.

She swallowed and bent down to stroke it, feeling much less as if she should take flight—the cat had obviously made the noise because there was no one else at home, simple, she told herself. And she flicked the torch on briefly again, before she stealthily made her way to the staircase and began to climb it one carpeted step at a time, counting beneath her breath and avoiding, from sheer habit, the fifteenth step that creaked.

Perhaps it was this that rendered her less cautious, she was to wonder later. Because to be silently enfolded into a pair of strong arms as she reached the top step took her supremely by surprise and paralyzed her for several heart-stopping moments. Then terror got the upper hand and she screamed and pummelled so vigorously, the two of them started to topple over in slow motion.

'Oh, no, you don't, lady!' she heard a masculine voice breathe huskily, but as she twisted like an eel she must have taken him by surprise, because the rest of what he'd been going to say was smothered by an exclamation of pain and she felt him go slack just long enough for her to evade his grasp, jump onto the banister and slide down it. Then she raced across the hall and kitchen, out through the laundry, locking the door with the key that was still in it, and sprinted across the back garden, jumped the fence and raced down the easement as if all the demons from hell were on her heels.

She'd had the foresight to park her car two blocks away. Although the easement led onto a different street from the front entrance to the house, she'd thought it wise in case anything went wrong and it could be identified. But, out of the heavily overcast sky, a clap of thunder at last rent the pregnant night and heavy rain began to fall.

'Thank you, thank you up there!' she whispered devoutly, although she was almost instantly soaked to the skin. 'A good storm has got to muddle my tracks, surely!'

'And just repeating the local headlines: the storm that ravaged the southern and bay-side suburbs of Brisbane last night is estimated to have caused close to a million dollars' damage to homes in its path... This is Aurora Templeton for Bay News.'

Aurora pulled off her headphones and steered her chair on its trolley tracks to the other end of the console. Her programme director gave her a thumbs-up sign and she got up stiffly and walked out of the studio. Her morning radio news shift was over and she couldn't be more grateful, not only because she felt as if she'd been through a wringer, but the consequences of her actions only hours ago had kicked in to plague her conscience with a vengeance.

She couldn't avoid looking around constantly or expecting a heavy hand to fall on her shoulder. And it had been the stuff nightmares were made of to wonder whether she would have to broadcast a police report of her own misdemeanour—thankfully not, but there was no guaranteeing it wouldn't be on tomorrow's news!

Why you never stop and think, Aurora Templeton, is a

mystery to me, she castigated herself bitterly and repeatedly on the way home.

Her new town house, in the Brisbane suburb of Manly, was pleasant and comfortable—or would be when she sorted the clutter.

Manly was an eastern suburb of Brisbane, south of the mouth of the Brisbane River on the shores of Moreton Bay. Because of its bay-side position, lovely breezes and views as well as its geographical make-up—a steep cliff running adjacent to the shore atop of which were some wonderful old houses—it had become fashionable again but it was also home to a large boat harbour.

Many of the boaties who enjoyed the waters of Moreton Bay, with its twin guardians of Moreton and North Stradbroke Islands, moored their boats in the Manly harbour so the suburb had a distinctly nautical flavour.

Aurora didn't have a view of the bay from her new town house although she did have a small garden and a courtyard. But she'd had no idea, when she'd come home a couple of weeks ago from six months overseas, that she'd find the family home sold, that her retired sea-captain father would have taken it into his head to buy a yacht and decide to sail around the world solo.

She'd lost her mother when she was six and been brought up by her father, when he'd been home, at boarding-school otherwise, and by a devoted housekeeper, Mrs Bunnings—known affectionately as 'Bunny'—in between times. But she'd also spent a lot of time travelling the world with her father and, at twenty-five, she had a Bachelor of Arts degree, she was fluent in several languages, cosmopolitan, well able to take care of herself and had embarked on a career in radio broadcasting.

None of that worldly education had managed to eradicate a daredevil streak in her character, however, which had often seen Bunny despair of her. And it was this that Aurora blamed as she brewed herself a cup of coffee in her new town house, the morning after she'd broken into Professor Luke Kirwan's home.

Well, not only that, she amended the thought as she inhaled the coffee aroma luxuriously. All sorts of things had gone towards creating the debacle, not the least her father's sudden decision to sell their home without even consulting her, then go sailing off into the wide blue yonder a bare few days after she'd got home and *before* she'd remembered her diaries.

She took her coffee to the lounge and curled up in a winged armchair, and thought back down the years.

She'd always been a compulsive scribbler, an inveterate diarist. Not that you would know it from the face she presented to the world but, deprived of her mother at an early age and separated from her father for long periods, an only child with no other close relatives—all of it had created the need in her for some kind of a lifeline, which was what her diaries had become: her companions that never deserted her.

The discovery, when she was about twelve, of a loose brick in the never-used fireplace of her bedroom that revealed a cavity in the wall behind it, had been a wonderful cache for them. She'd used it right up until she'd gone overseas, convinced her dreams, fantasies and innermost thoughts were quite safe from prying eyes.

But it wasn't until she'd rung Bunny to tell her that she was home and to discuss the turmoil of Ambrose Templeton's unexpected actions that she'd remembered them.

Bunny had been delighted to hear from her and able to tell her that she had been kept on, three mornings a week, as a cleaner for the new owner of Aurora's old home. That was when a vision of the fireplace in her old bedroom had floated through Aurora's mind and her mouth had dropped open...

It hadn't taken long to occur to her, however, that the

normal course of action, simply ringing the new owner and explaining about secret caches and diaries, was, at the same time, inviting extreme curiosity in any normal person who most probably would not be able to resist having a look first for themselves... Just thinking about it made her break out in a cold sweat.

So she'd rung up and tried to make an appointment with Professor Luke Kirwan, Professor of Physics, she now knew, without giving a reason other than saying it was important and personal, and with the thinking that, once she was in the house, she could explain then and retrieve her diaries herself so that no one could get to them first.

Only to discover that the professor himself didn't take calls at home at all. He had an extremely officious secretary to do it for him during working hours, long working hours at that, and an answering machine he never responded to at other times.

Nor was this secretary—and Bunny had told her what a dragon the woman was, always sneaking up behind her to check what she was doing—at all interested in making an appointment for Aurora with the professor without good reason, saying he was far too busy at the moment unless she could state her case.

Aurora had thought swiftly, then explained that she was the previous owner's daughter, she'd been away at the time of the sale and she'd just like to check that nothing of hers had been left behind.

'Definitely not,' Miss Dragon Hillier had said coldly down the line. 'I checked the house myself and you can rest assured there was nothing that shouldn't be here! Good day.' And she'd put the phone down heavily.

Aurora had taken the receiver from her ear and breathed fierily. But she'd forced herself to calm down and devise Plan B. Of course! She would simply roll up, after office hours, and corner the professor in his den without his dragon lady protector. But this professor of physics had proved to be extremely elusive. She'd rolled up to her old address five times in as many days to find no one home. The fifth time had been when the germ of an idea had started to niggle at the back of her mind.

'What's he like?' she'd asked Bunny, over the phone. It had occurred to her to ask Bunny to get her diaries for her, but she'd discarded the idea immediately on the grounds that she could lose Bunny her job—especially since Miss Hillier was a such a sticky beak. But would a few simple questions do any harm? she'd pondered.

'Don't know, I've never met him, only the dragon, she hired me on your father's recommendation,' Bunny had replied. 'And he's always gone by the time I get to work and doesn't seem to come home during the day. Mind you, it's only been a few weeks, but I'll tell you what, love, I think he's a regular old fuddy-duddy. She's certainly as fussy as can be and I guess it comes from him!'

'Has he made any changes, Bunny?' Aurora had asked a little hesitantly. 'And has he got a wife or—'

'Nope, he's a bachelor. Can't for the life of me understand why he wants to rattle about in a house that size—he doesn't even have a dog, although there is a cat. As for changes, none so far although I heard her talking to a builder on the phone to get a quote to brick up the fireplaces in the bedrooms, the ones your dad always used to say were such a waste in a climate like Brisbane.'

Aurora had almost dropped the phone. 'I see,' she'd said rather hollowly.

'You OK, pet?' Bunny had enquired, then continued without waiting for an answer, 'Must say the place is beautifully furnished, lots of antiques that take a powerful lot of dusting, mind. You would think he'd have a dog to guard it all, especially as he's away an awful lot, apparently. I also heard her book him an air ticket to Perth for next weekend, flying out Friday, coming back Monday, but they didn't even change the locks as new owners often like to do. I guess the old place is pretty hard to get into when you stop to think about it, though.'

'Yes.' Aurora had swallowed. 'Yes.' And she'd let Bunny ramble on for a few minutes more before ending the conversation. Then she'd up-ended the contents of the suitcases Bunny had packed with her clothes and personal possessions that had come from the house, and fallen on an old wallet to find her laundry door key still sitting snugly in a zip-up compartment...

She came back to the present with a sigh. She still might not have done it if she hadn't rung once more and tried again to get past Miss Hillier, this time to be told flatly that the professor was busier than ever and would she please stop bothering them! There'd also been a curious innuendo in the other woman's scathing tones that she'd been unable to pin down but it was almost as if she, Aurora, should be ashamed of herself for some reason—it was this strange insinuation that had added fuel to the flames and made her decide to take things into her own hands.

So what to do now? she wondered. Would the professor and his dragon lady secretary associate her calls with this home invasion? Should she step forward and confess?

The phone rang as she was thinking these thoughts and it was Bunny, deliciously full of news. Believe it or not, the professor had been robbed! Well, Bunny had gone on to explain, he'd come home early from Perth on account of some virulent bug that had laid him low and put himself straight to bed, only to wake around midnight ravaged by a headache and thirst. He'd stepped out of his bedroom, stood for a few minutes wondering where the light switch was as often happened to people in new homes, then, despite feeling extremely groggy and unwell, had noticed a strange light at the bottom of the stairs.

And, when someone had begun to ascend the stairs, between wondering whether he was hallucinating and defi-

nitely not feeling well enough to grapple with a
stayed quite silent until the intruder had literally w
his waiting arms—only to knock himself out briefly
ensuing mêlée.

'You don't…say!' Aurora commented feebly at this fir.
break in Bunny's narrative. 'Is…is he all right? Was anything stolen?' she forced herself to add.

No, nothing was missing, Bunny reported, but that could
have been because the intruder had been disturbed; no, he
was back in bed but mainly because of a virus he'd picked
up and—here Bunny chuckled—would you believe it? He'd
actually left the front door ajar when he'd come home which
was, according to the police, tantamount to issuing any stray
burglar who happened to be 'out and about casing joints' an
open invitation!

'How…bizarre!'

Bunny agreed, still chuckling. 'Talk about the absent-
minded professor! Although, he was pretty crook.'

'So…so what are the police going to do?' Aurora asked.

'Well, love, there've been a few burglaries in the area,
apparently, and they suspect there's a bit of a gang at work,
must have been them, they reckon, but they didn't sound
too hopeful of pinning them down on this one. In all the
chaos of the storm—we got three broken windows and the
garden is kind of flattened—they can't find any evidence of
anyone being on the property.'

Aurora swallowed, mainly with relief, as Bunny chatted
on about how she'd been given the day off. And when
Aurora finally put the phone down, she thought she might
have had a very lucky escape; she told herself she would
never do anything as foolish again, but there still remained
the problem of her diaries…

It took her a week to acknowledge that she would either
have to come clean with the professor and resign herself to
either he or Miss Hillier reading them before she got to

em, or resign herself to having them bricked up for ever, assuming the builder doing the bricking up didn't find them.

Then, out of the blue, came a ray of light. Her programme director, Neil Baker, asked her if she'd like to accompany him to a house-warming party. They'd actually met overseas and laughed at one of life's little coincidences that they should be working together back in 'Oz', but there'd never been any romantic spark between them.

'You wouldn't be between girlfriends, Neil?' she teased.

He grimaced and confessed that he was, but he'd been invited to bring a partner to this party, to which his ex-girlfriend had *also* been invited, and... He paused and looked awkward.

'OK, I get the picture.' Aurora grinned. 'Where and when?'

'Luke Kirwan has got himself a new pad, somewhere up on the hill. Know him?'

Aurora coughed to cover her start of surprise. 'Er...no. You do, I gather?'

'Yep. I was at uni with him. Like to come? It's this Friday night, semi-formal and I'll take the present.'

'I...yes.'

The thing was to look as little as possible like a cat burglar, Aurora told herself as she studied her wardrobe early on Friday evening.

Of course, it would be even better if she could persuade herself to come down with a sudden bout of flu and give up the whole idea of going to this party at all, but...

She flicked back her long streaky fair hair and planted her hands on her hips. Who did this professor and his watchdog secretary think they were? Common courtesy alone was entirely absent from their behaviour and if they thought they could brush her aside like a troublesome, somehow rather shameful fly, they could think again. She would go and, if the opportunity presented itself, she would retrieve her diaries.

She chose a flamenco outfit she'd picked up in Spain, a long flounced skirt with pink flowers on a dark background and a white blouse. She pinned a fake pink gardenia into her hair and studied her reflection.

It was almost a boyish little face beneath the glorious hair but redeemed by a pair of thickly lashed, sparkling green eyes that were little short of sensational. At barely five feet two, her figure was neat, compact and very slim.

She started to smile at herself in the long mirror as she kicked the skirt aside and raised her hands above her head—it was a beautiful outfit and she always felt wonderful in it. As if she could dance the flamenco all night but, not only that, even without her mantilla, she always felt as if the clothes and the dance were a sensuous celebration of her femininity.

She lowered her arms abruptly—perhaps those were not the right vibes to be giving off at Professor Luke Kirwan's house-warming? Perhaps she should dress to be as inconspicuous as possible rather than trying to look the opposite to a cat burglar? She frowned, then shrugged as the doorbell rang—it was too late to change now.

'Wow!' Neil Baker looked suitably impressed. 'You look absolutely stunning, Aurora.'

'Thanks.' She got into his car and stowed her fringed shoulder bag at her feet. It was a little bulkier than normal because it contained a green rubbish bag and a length of strong fishing line as well as her lipstick, comb and a hanky. She smiled at Neil as he started the engine for the short drive to her old home. 'Tell me a bit about this friend of yours?'

'He's really brilliant, but he's a good bloke for all that. There was a rumour that he and a girl called Leonie Murdoch were about to get hitched—maybe this is a surprise engagement party too,' Neil theorized, 'because I can't see why he needs a house otherwise. There's a hell of a lot of old money in the family, family homes and a sheep station out west—here we are!'

Aurora opened her mouth as she stared at her *old* family home lit up most attractively tonight, and it was on the tip of her tongue to tell Neil that she was no stranger to this house and why, just in case she met someone she knew, but the moment seemed to pass without her being able to get it out. Then she saw how many people were streaming into this house-warming party, and it didn't seem to matter—she would only be one insignificant guest in a big crowd.

But once she was inside, she did take the precaution of asking Neil to point Luke Kirwan out to her because she had every intention of avoiding their host as much as was possible. Only Miss Hillier, fortyish, upright, groomed within an inch of life and looking every bit the martinet she sounded, had been at the door to greet guests.

'Uh…' Neil looked around the throng as glasses of champagne were pressed upon them—a catering firm had obviously been hired '…oh, there he is! Over by the piano. I think I'll wait until things settle down rather than fight through the crowd to introduce you, if that's OK with you?' he added, but rather distractedly as he scanned the throng intently.

'Fine!' Aurora said, more enthusiastically than was called for, as she gazed through the crowd at the man beside the piano. Actually there were two, but one of them wore thick glasses, had thinning fair hair, was short and wore an Argyle tie with a mustard corduroy shirt beneath a baggy tweed jacket. He also had a pipe in his hand.

No one could possibly look more 'donnish', she decided and smiled inwardly. So that was Professor Luke Kirwan. No wonder he had to employ a dragon lady to run things for him because he literally exuded the kind of fuddy-duddy ineffectualness one associated with an absent-minded professor.

Which was not how you could describe the man standing next to him, she mused as she felt herself relaxing beneath the vastly less than threatening presence of the man she'd grappled with at the top of the stairs on that never-to-be-forgotten night.

No, another kettle of fish altogether, the second man beside the piano. In fact, downright arresting might be a good way to put it, she decided.

Tall with brushed-back dark hair, he had a wide brow, smooth skin, high cheekbones and slight hollows beneath those good bones as his face tapered to a hard mouth and a jaw-line that indicated this was not a man to trifle with. He also had dark, brooding eyes and he was leaning negligently against the baby grand looking cool, slightly bored and capable of a rather damning kind of arrogance if he chose.

From what she could see, he wore indigo designer jeans, a midnight-blue shirt beneath a faultlessly tailored navy jacket and a shot-silk amethyst tie. He also had a glass of something in his hands which he twirled now and then before putting it to his lips, draining it and setting it down decisively. As he straightened and his dark gaze roamed around the crowded room briefly, she saw that he was even taller than she'd suspected with wide shoulders.

Well, well, Aurora found herself thinking as that indifferent gaze failed to be impressed by anything it saw and he turned away—what have we here? A hawk amongst the sparrows? A real man amongst us? I wonder what he does for a living? Could he be a corsair in disguise, a better-looking, more dangerous James Bond than any of them, a modern-day Mr Darcy?

This time an outward smile twisted her lips because it was just that typical flight of fantasy that made it so difficult for her to allow anyone to read her diaries...

Over the next two hours, the party got noisier and merrier. She also got separated from Neil, who still hadn't got around to introducing her to Luke Kirwan for the simple reason that as soon as he and his ex-girlfriend laid eyes on each other, they were drawn together like a pin to a magnet and determined, it appeared, to have things out with each other despite being in the middle of a party.

'Look,' Neil said awkwardly to Aurora as his ex-girlfriend glowered at her over her shoulder, 'I'm sorry about this but—'

'Forget about me, Neil.' Aurora chuckled. 'If looks could kill I should be six feet under by now, which tells me she's still very interested in you, so go for it! I can take care of myself.'

Neil looked both grateful and exasperated at the same time, but, five minutes later, neither of them were to be sighted.

Aurora shrugged, still amused but also aware that she was a free agent now, which simplified things considerably. She could put her plan—of wandering upstairs in search of a powder room but nipping into her old bedroom to get her diaries—into action, and she could leave the party whenever it suited her without anyone being the wiser.

Before she got to implement any of it, though, she'd wandered outside onto the terrace to drink in the view she knew so well and loved—the Manly Boat Harbour by night with its millions of dollars' worth of yachts and all kinds of small crafts tied up to the jetties—when a disco struck up on the terrace and couples drifted out to dance.

And she was actually thinking that this was a livelier kind of party than one would expect of an absent-minded professor when a deep voice behind her drawled, 'May I have this dance, señorita?'

For some reason the hairs on the nape of her neck stood up as she turned slowly, then she knew why—it was the man who'd been standing beside the professor at the piano.

She took an unexpected breath to be on the receiving end of that dark, worldly gaze, but said lightly, 'Oh, it's you.'

He raised an eyebrow. 'You were expecting me?'

'Not at all, señor.' She smiled faintly. 'I got the rather strong impression not much about this party was of any interest to you.'

A glint of something like mockery entered his dark eyes. 'When did you get that impression?'

She shook out her hair and opted for honesty against confusion at being caught in having 'sized him up', so to speak. 'When you were leaning against the piano looking bored,' she said with a glimmer of mischief curving her lips.

'That must have been before I caught sight of you,' he countered, then frowned slightly. 'Are you—unaccompanied?'

'I am now, although I didn't start out that way.' She looked wry. 'My escort met his ex-girlfriend and they've disappeared. I'm not sure if they're making up or tearing each other to bits, but something intensely dramatic was going on between them so I decided to withdraw rather than get my eyes scratched out.'

'Then he wasn't the love of your life?'

'No way. I was only filling in *because* they'd split up!'

'I think he needs his head read,' the man remarked thoughtfully. 'Do you dance, señorita? It would be a pity not to do that gorgeous outfit justice.' His gaze roamed up and down her figure.

'That's what I always think when I'm wearing it,' Aurora replied simply, although conscious of a tremor running through her, sparked by that heavy-lidded dark gaze on her body. And she knew instinctively that her sensuous pleasure in herself, brought on by this outfit, had communicated itself to this stranger—in other words it had been a mistake to wear it. But how was she to have known she would bump into the one man who would sense that, where others mightn't?

She also caught herself thinking that this stranger was

dynamite, and she should possibly exercise due caution or she might find herself willingly led down the garden path...

That was nonsense, she immediately corrected the thought, another flight of sheer fantasy! All the same, it wouldn't go astray to take care.

She said, whimsically, 'I won't treat you to a full flamenco, though.'

'Could you?'

'I took lessons in Spain a few months ago. They called me the pocket señorita.'

He studied her upturned face until she moved restlessly beneath the way his gaze took in her eyes, then rested squarely on her mouth before he said pensively, 'Why do I get the feeling you could be a pocket dynamo all round, Miss...?'

But Aurora, who found her heart beating abnormally and her senses all at sixes and sevens beneath not only the way this man was looking at her but everything about him, clutched a straw of sanity. 'I'd rather remain anonymous at the moment,' she said with a delicious look of fun in her eyes. 'If you don't tread on my toes or have sweaty palms I might reconsider, but I'm not promising anything.'

He didn't reply, only inclined his head, took her in his arms and swung her into the beat of the music. Then he stopped and frowned down at her again, but only for a moment before he rather absently steered her through the dancers.

As for Aurora, she also found herself dancing mechanically for several reasons. A determination not to be overly impressed by this man on such short notice, but also because of a prickling sense of *déjà vu*. Why, though? she wondered. She was quite sure she'd never met him before—he was not the kind of man you forgot—so it had to be because she was back on the terrace of her old home, only—that didn't seem to fit.

'Have I offended some other, unnamed principle of yours,

Miss Anonymous? Body odour or bad breath?' he drawled, breaking her out of her frowning reverie.

Her eyes widened. 'Uh…no, sorry, nothing like that at all! You smell quite nice in a manly way.' She inhaled delicately. 'I'm not partial to overpowering aftershave or cologne on men.'

'Neither am I,' he said abruptly. 'You, on the other hand, use a particularly delicate, floral perfume.'

'Thank you! It is rather nice, isn't it? I have it specially made up for me by a friend who is into that kind of thing.'

'So it's—uniquely yours?' There was a rather intent little gleam in his eyes as he asked the question.

'Yes. Do you have a problem with that?' she asked curiously.

'No. Why should I?'

'I don't know. You just looked a bit—' she shrugged '—censorious about my perfume.'

He smiled faintly. 'I think it all goes towards making you rather special.' He held her away and looked down at her consideringly before raising his eyes to hers. 'Do you have anyone in your life—when you're not helping hapless men friends out?'

Aurora, once more clasped in his arms, began to dance again. 'I don't think we know each other well enough to go into that. Unless you'd like to set the ball rolling by telling me about your love life?' She raised an eyebrow delicately at him.

'In point of fact I happen to be—unattached at the moment,' he responded gravely.

'And on the prowl,' Aurora suggested with an undercurrent of irony.

'What makes you think that?'

'Could be that my antennae are picking up those vibes about you,' she replied ingenuously. 'In fact, I warned myself to be on guard against being led down the garden path not long after we started to dance.'

He laughed, and there was something curiously breathtaking about it despite Aurora's wish to be unimpressed by him. Because it revealed a vitality that made you want to laugh too, and made you want to get to know this man, who could be so damningly bored at times then respond so fascinatingly to something you'd said—so that you felt absolutely fascinated yourself.

'I have yet to resort to leading a girl down the garden path,' he denied, 'although the opposite may not be true.'

Aurora blinked and wrinkled her brow. 'You have a problem with girls leading *you* down the garden path?'

'Occasionally.'

They danced in silence for a while as Aurora digested this. She wasn't sure if he was serious, although it was not hard to imagine him cutting a swathe through the female population. She said, eventually, 'How old are you?'

He looked briefly taken aback. 'Thirty-seven, why?'

She smiled wisely. 'Then it's about time you got yourself a wife, I would think, not only to keep *you* on the straight and narrow but to discourage women from making fools of themselves over you.'

'Are you suggesting yourself for the position?' he came back smoothly and with a mocking little smile playing on his lips.

'Not at all,' Aurora replied airily. 'I plan to have a lot more fun and adventure before I embark on marriage, domesticity and maternity.'

'And do you think these things work to plan?' he queried, rather dryly, she thought.

'For me they do—so far, anyway!'

'How nice,' he commented, and said no more for a time.

But it was not long before Aurora realised, as they danced, that it was far easier said than done to remain impervious to this man. He danced well, holding her lightly and certainly not imposing any unwelcome familiarities on her. In fact he was being a very correct partner—but that could be a mockery, she found herself thinking darkly.

There was certainly a quizzical gleam in his eyes from time to time as he so carefully observed the proprieties. Almost as if he knew exactly, damn him, how wonderful he was to dance with even so correctly. How easily his well-knit body moved to the rhythm—how impossible it was not to feel rather stunningly aware of him even held so lightly in his arms.

'You were thinking?' he murmured, his dark eyes resting wickedly on her flushed face, after he'd twirled her expertly so that her skirt belled out beautifully, and brought her back safely into his arms.

'That's for me to know and you to ponder upon,' she replied, and was annoyed to hear herself sounding defensive.

'Then I'll tell you what *I* was thinking, Miss Anonymous. That we dance so well together, there are certain other—activities,' he said, barely audibly, 'we should be able to lend ourselves to excellently.'

Aurora took a breath and felt her cheeks redden, but she was unable to prevent herself from replying in kind as anger also coursed through her veins. 'Really?' she said gently. 'I should warn you that I don't take my clothes off on first encounters.'

He took the opportunity to look right through her clothes, then raised a lazy eyebrow at her. 'A pity, but it might create a riot here and now, wouldn't you agree?'

'Perhaps I should rephrase,' Aurora started to say.

He laughed softly. 'Perhaps. That is cutting to the chase rather rapidly.'

'You started this,' she reminded him, trying valiantly to sound cool and unflustered, although she was kicking herself mentally.

'I may have,' he agreed, 'but I was thinking along the lines of extending the pleasure we take in dancing with each other...' he paused and looked down at her significantly until she had to look away with a mixture of embarrassment and self-directed ire '…to another, quite lovely level that wouldn't, however, require us to undress.'

Aurora missed her step and marvelled bitterly at the ease with which he redirected her to the rhythm. And it was impossible not to silently contemplate another 'lovely level' with this man, right there as she was, in his arms, with their bodies touching when the music brought them together.

It should be impossible, she mused. She was not an impressionable girl, she was not particularly naïve, but she had the distinct feeling that this man had somehow got past her defences with his mixture of intriguing looks, his arrogantly bored air and his exquisitely polite handling of her that, at the same time, had activated all sorts of reactions in her. Nor did his approach—guaranteed, one would have thought, to prove she was being 'toyed' with—stop her from wondering what it would be like to be somewhere private with him.

What would happen? she even found herself wondering. Would she allow herself to be kissed—the next level he appeared to have in mind? Would she be able to resist if he was as good at it as he was to dance with?

She stopped dancing abruptly and looked at him lethally. 'All right, you've had your bit of fun. I think we should part company now.'

'Why? Didn't you tell me you were into "fun" for a good while yet?' His gaze rested pointedly on the curve of her breasts beneath her blouse, then flicked up to her eyes with a mixture of derision and irony.

Aurora compressed her lips and took hold. Enough of this, she told herself. She'd come here for one reason tonight and it certainly wasn't to get waylaid by a man, however gorgeous. Make that downright *dangerous*, she reflected with an inward little shiver. And as the music changed it presented her with the perfect escape.

'Fun—oh, yes! Let's see if you can really dance,' she teased, and whirled herself out of his arms as the rhythm changed and she started to do the twist expertly along with the rest of the dancers.

When it came to an end, everyone was hot and laughing and fanning themselves, but her partner took her hand and said, 'Well? Do I qualify to get your name now?'

'Tell you what,' she suggested, 'I really need to powder my nose. If you could find me a long, cool drink in the meantime, who knows?' And she regained her hand and melted away into the crowd. A quick peep over her shoulder once she was inside told her that another woman had claimed him.

All the better, she thought as she found her bag, unobtrusively scanned the staircase and, seeing it deserted, slipped upstairs. No one knew better than she that there was a downstairs powder room for just these occasions, but surely a guest in a supposedly strange house could be forgiven for going upstairs?

And, in the proverbial twinkling of an eye, she'd let herself into her old bedroom. The room was in darkness but she waited for a few minutes, then moved forward cautiously, feeling for the bed and finding a bedside table. She had her hand on what felt like a lamp when the door opened and the overhead light went on. She froze, then swung round to see the man she'd danced with anonymously standing in the doorway.

'So,' he said with soft but unmistakable menace, closing the door behind him without turning, 'I was right.'

'I...I...' Aurora stammered '...I...was looking for a bathroom. I couldn't seem to find the light, that's all.'

He smiled grimly. 'Again? I'm only surprised you didn't bring your torch with you, Little Miss Spain, who didn't want to tell me her name.'

Aurora blinked and licked her lips. 'I don't know what you mean.' She backed away as he moved towards her, and sat down unexpectedly on the bed. 'I don't know what you're doing here either. Please leave, and I'll find the bathroom on my own.'

'Give me one good reason for *not* telling me your name,' he countered.

She swallowed and thought frantically, then decided that the closer she could stick to the truth, the better. She tossed her hair with more spirit than she actually felt. 'I don't believe in being bowled over by men on first encounters.'

'As in allowing yourself to be attracted to them even when it's already happened?' he suggested, with a wealth of satire in his dark gaze. 'Or wearing provocative outfits,' he added meaningfully.

Damn, Aurora thought, that hadn't been such a good idea after all; and could think of nothing to say, so she merely shrugged.

'But tonight was our second encounter, wasn't it?' he drawled then. 'Aren't you forgetting the way we...bumped into each other at the top of the stairs the last time you invaded my home?'

Aurora's mouth fell open and her eyes were suddenly huge. '*Your* home! Who...who are you?' she said in a strangled kind of croak.

'Luke Kirwan,' he replied, looking altogether taller, tougher and much more dangerous than she'd imagined earlier. 'And you're not getting out of here until you tell me what you're so determined to steal from me, señorita.'

CHAPTER TWO

'YOU can't be!' Aurora gasped, absolutely thunderstruck.

He studied her narrowly. 'Believe me, I am. And this is *my* house, in case you've devised a ploy to confuse things somehow or other.'

'But…but…who's the other one, then?' she stammered.

'Other what?'

'The man you were standing with next to the piano—the man who looks just like a prof—' She broke off and bit her lip.

Luke Kirwan frowned and she saw him concentrate for a moment, then look fleetingly amused. 'Jack Barnard?' he suggested. 'He's my solicitor, but what has that got to do with any of this, señorita?' he enquired coldly.

Aurora swallowed painfully and closed her eyes as she grappled not only with the folly of judging people on their appearances, but also having that prickling sense of *déjà vu* explained to her in this manner. She had been in Luke Kirwan's arms before—not for long before she'd started to pummel and struggle with him, but long enough, obviously, for it to have imprinted itself on her subconscious.

But, it suddenly occurred to her and she clasped her hands together tightly, if that was all *he* had to go on, a similar sense of *déjà vu*, then he didn't have a leg to stand on…

'I think I know what's going through your head, my pretty,' he drawled as her lashes flew up. 'How do I know it was you at the top of the stairs the last time you tried to rob me? I'll tell you. Same height, same petite figure, same…' he paused and looked wry '…athleticism but, above all, same unique—as you told me yourself—perfume.' His dark eyes glinted sardonically.

Aurora's lips parted and her eyes widened. Then she closed them again and barely stopped herself from saying caustically that, for a man groggy with some kind of virus, he'd taken in an awful lot about her and no one would buy it anyway!

But he spoke again, and this time there was a grim warning underlying his words that caused her to tremble inwardly. 'Of course, finding you creeping around my bedroom, when there's a clear sign downstairs directing people to a *downstairs* bathroom, adds a lot more weight to my evidence, don't you agree?'

Aurora looked around properly for the first time. It had never occurred to her that the new owner would not use the master bedroom, but that was exactly what Luke Kirwan appeared to have done. Her old bedroom was now definitely, although luxuriously, furnished for a man.

'I preferred the view from this room,' he said, as if reading her thoughts.

Damn, she thought again, and forcibly prevented herself from wiping her face.

'Well, Mr Kirwan,' she said after a moment's thought, 'I am sorry for inadvertently invading your bedroom but you're mistaken. I didn't see the sign downstairs so it couldn't have been so very clear. As for all the rest of it, whatever it is, I...' she tilted her chin and gazed at him imperiously '...I'm happy to forget about it if you would be so kind as to direct me to a bathroom. I'll even leave your party then, since you cherish these amazing suspicions about me. In fact, nothing would induce me to stay,' she finished proudly.

He laughed softly as he took in the hauteur of her expression, the set of her small chin, her very straight back and the outraged bearing of her slender figure—even seated on a bed. 'You're a rather brilliant actress, aren't you?' he commented. 'But the only thing that's going to get you out of here is telling me who you are and *why* you're here—'

'I've told you that!' she interrupted.

'So you have. It doesn't wash, though.' He studied her comprehensively, right through her clothes again, in fact, so that she started to boil beneath that dark, insolently intimate gaze. 'What is beginning to wash is something a little different,' he continued leisurely. 'Could you even be a groupie, señorita, who devised a rather novel way of getting through my secretary's net?'

Aurora's mouth fell open. 'I have no idea what you're talking about!'

'No?' The scepticism in his expression was chilling. 'Never heard of student groupies? Girls? Believe me, it's an occupation for some of them; it would appear to be the only reason they're at university in the first place,' he said with damning scorn.

Several things suddenly came clear to Aurora, including his secretary's manner and why he never answered the phone himself, but the shock of it all rendered her speechless.

Giving him the opportunity to continue with lethal satire, 'Why, yes. Heaven alone knows what bizarre scheme you'd concocted the other night—looking for something to steal from me to blackmail me into bed with you, perhaps?' He raised an eyebrow at her. 'But your actions tonight have been loud and clear—coyly refusing to tell me your name, being a seductively mysterious guest—and so on,' he finished flatly.

To be thought of as a coy, student groupie throwing herself at his feet in a rather 'novel' manner caused Aurora to lose her temper completely. 'Look here—' she bounced off the bed '—I've had enough of this. Will you get out of my way before I scream the place down?'

'Scream away,' he invited. 'The only thing that will achieve is to have me call the police.'

'*What?*'

'Oh, yes,' he said. 'In fact, you have a choice. I'll leave

you here for a period of sober reflection. When I come back, either you tell me the truth or I do get the police.'

'If you think I have any intention of staying here,' she spat at him, 'you're mistaken!'

'No, I'm not. I propose to lock you in, you see.'

Aurora flew at him, prepared to scratch his eyes out, only to find herself caught in a grip of steel. 'Let me go!' she gasped through pale lips.

'I'd rather let an enraged tigress go.' He pinioned her hands behind her back. 'I've also got something of a score to settle with you, Miss Spain. Let's see if you kiss as well as you do—other things.'

'I never kiss under these circumstances. I'm perfectly capable of biting, however,' she warned through her teeth.

He smiled crookedly. 'What circumstances do you kiss under?'

'I need to be in love or on the way to it, like any normal girl,' she replied scathingly. 'The last thing I can imagine with you, Professor. For one thing, you're too old for me, for another the mere thought of doing it under duress turns me right off!' Her green eyes were proud and defiant.

'OK.' He released her pinioned hands but transferred his hands to her waist. 'In exchange for no duress, could I get a promise that you'll keep your fists to yourself?'

'I'm not promising anything!'

'Then how about…' there was the glint of wicked amusement in his dark eyes although he spoke gravely '…proving to me that I am too old for you?'

'You must think I'm still in my cradle,' Aurora retorted, 'to fall for that old line!'

'On the contrary, before I discovered you sneaking around my bedroom, I thought you were gorgeous, certainly of the age of consent—' his gaze roamed up and down her figure '—and quite stunning.'

Aurora's lips parted and, before she could think of a suitable rejoinder, he drew her into his arms. She breathed once, jerkily, but, to her horror, the spell of Luke Kirwan once again began to weave itself around her. And no twelve-year age difference was going to save her, she realised—not that she'd said it as anything but a crushing, heat-of-the-moment snub.

To make things worse, she also realized from the smile twisting his lips that her thought processes were about as easy for him to read as an open book. 'Look,' she began uneasily, 'this is insane! You can't just do it...'

'I can and I'm going to, so save your breath,' he recommended. 'Don't tell me there isn't the slightest curiosity on your side?'

He moved his hands on her hips and she went to say something, stopped with her lips parted as all sorts of sensations started to run through her—and not only physical. Knowing that part of the dangerous attraction of this man for her was that she was playing with fire, for example. *See if you can be unaffected by this, Little Miss Spain,* she mimicked in her mind, because she had no doubt that was the gauntlet Luke Kirwan was throwing down. But it would be madness to take it up...

He did it for her. He took advantage of her confusion to withdraw his hands from her hips and cup her face lightly at the same time as he captured her green gaze so that she was unable to look away. 'Small, neat and stylish—whatever else it is you are, my would-be robber, and, I suspect, delicious. Let's see.' He lowered his head.

Aurora trembled as his lips touched hers, but he said against the corner of her mouth, 'I was right: sweet as a peach, señorita.' And started to kiss her properly.

The crazy part about it was that he made her feel as sweet as a peach while he kissed her lingeringly, but not only that. He himself felt so amazingly good it was almost impossible to remain unaffected. How did he do it? she marvelled as he ran his hands down her back and laid a trail of featherlight kisses down her neck. With great restraint, she answered herself. This was no stolen, victory kiss—he was far too clever for that, damn him, she thought.

This was a skilled assault that made her skin feel like silk as those cool, dry lips wandered across it, and the way his hands found the curves of her body made her heartbeat triple. This was a man who made not one blunder while her senses rioted and she began to drink in the feel of him through her pores.

His height, those broad shoulders, the interesting hollows of his face, which she found herself wanting to touch, the crisp cotton of his shirt, the hard, taut length of him that she was now resting against as he stopped kissing her, with not an ounce of defiance left in her but one embarrassingly girlish word on her lips—Wow!

To her everlasting gratitude, she managed to stop herself from actually saying it as he put her away from him and steadied her before releasing her.

'Well?' There was sheer devilry in those dark eyes as he posed the question.

Aurora breathed deeply and had to suffer the indignity of him restoring some tendrils of hair behind her ears and straightening the collar of her blouse before she could think of a response. Then she could only fall back on the truth. 'I'm speechless,' she said huskily and licked her lips.

He raised an eyebrow at her with a mixture of amusement and mockery. 'I'll take it as read, then. And I'll leave you to—compose yourself.'

'I didn't necessarily mean I was bowled over or anything...' she began to protest not quite truthfully, but stopped with her eyes darkening. 'You're not still going to lock me in!'

'Oh, yes, I am, sweetheart,' he said coolly, then looked amused. 'By the way, there's an *en*-suite bathroom through there.' He pointed. 'Never let it be said I inconvenienced a guest even if they are burglars or groupies—and I'm now quite sure it was you that dark and stormy night.' He turned on his heel and walked out and Aurora heard the key turn in the lock before she was able to think of a thing to do.

'I don't *believe* this!' she said through gritted teeth, then sank back onto the bed to drop her face into her hands as she marvelled bitterly on her sheer bad luck and wondered what to do next. Of course, it was obvious, she thought. She had no choice but to come clean, yet it went supremely against the grain to be outwitted by this man and there was no guarantee he wouldn't insist on reading at least some bits of her diaries...

Several minutes later she got up and went into the bathroom, where she washed her face and had a drink of water. Then she returned to the bedroom and went straight to the fireplace. The brick came out easily; her diaries were still in the cache. She removed them, put them into the plastic bag from her shoulder bag and tied the fishing line to the bag. She turned off the light and went to the window that was so impossible to climb out of because of the wrought-iron bars—apart from being one floor above the ground.

Five minutes of silent, intense scrutiny of the shrubbery and surrounds below yielded nothing, no movement at all. Her old bedroom was not directly above any window on the ground floor, so she felt quite safe as she manoeuvred the rubbish bag awkwardly through the bars, lowered it to the ground to be swallowed up amongst some flourishing hydrangea bushes, and threw the line down after it.

Then she switched on the light again and looked around. Despite the luxuriousness of the bedroom, a thick-pile silvery blue carpet, matching curtains and bed cover, there was only one chair, a wooden antique that matched the marvellous bureau but looked highly uncomfortable.

She shrugged, slipped her shoes off and retired to Luke Kirwan's bed, where she propped the pillows up behind her and picked up the book on his bedside table—a murder mystery, as it happened. And she'd finished the first chapter when she heard the key in the lock. She made no move to get up and that was his first sight of her as he came into the room—propped against his pillows, looking gravely at him over the top of his book.

Inwardly, Luke Kirwan was amused. This girl had enormous nerve if nothing else. Not that she lacked other qualities, he conceded. A delicate figure, unusual beauty—her hair and eyes alone were stunning—a flair for clothes and the kind of *joie de vivre* that was infectious. The fact remained, he reminded himself, that discreet enquiries downstairs had shed no light on who she was, and the story of coming with someone who'd deserted her for an ex-girlfriend was most likely another invention.

'I do hope you're comfortable—or, after what passed in here before I locked you in, is that an invitation to join you?' he said with an undercurrent of sarcasm.

'Not at all.' Aurora closed the book, got up and slipped on her shoes. She added, as she shook out her beautiful skirt and ran her hands through her hair, 'It was your idea to lock me in, not mine, so I couldn't see why I shouldn't make myself comfortable. How do you do, by the way? I'm Aurora Templeton.' She held out her hand.

He crossed the room to take it, and felt it tremble briefly in his. It was the only sign of inner nerves he could detect, however. Her back was as straight as ever, her chin elevated and those stunning green eyes proud.

'Why do I get the feeling this is not to be a—*penitent* confession—brought on by sober reflection?' he murmured a little wryly.

Aurora took her hand back. 'Because you really have only yourself to blame, Mr Kirwan. You and your secretary, that is. This preoccupation with guarding you from "groupies" is what brought this all about. I find it a little hard to believe that any kind of a real man needs to go to those lengths anyway, but, be that as it may—if I could have got in touch with you by any other means, I would not have had to resort to this.'

'Hang on—resort to robbing me, do you mean?' he queried quizzically.

'No. Reclaiming my property,' she stated.

'Really, you're going to have explain better than that, Aurora Templeton.' He paused and narrowed his eyes. 'Why does that name ring a bell?'

'From the number of messages I left on your answering machine that you ignored?' she suggested with irony. 'But you also bought this house from my father,' she explained. 'This was my bedroom.'

Luke Kirwan blinked.

'And this,' Aurora continued, turning towards the fireplace, 'was my secret cache from the time I discovered it when I was about twelve.'

He followed her across the room and ducked his head to look into the fireplace. He observed the brick and the empty cavity in the wall, put his hand into it and whistled softly. 'I see,' he said as he straightened.

'Good!' Aurora said briskly. 'Now, you may or may not have been aware that I was overseas at the time the house was sold—'

'I had no idea Ambrose Templeton had a daughter,' he said, and pulled a handkerchief from his pocket to wipe his hands.

'Well, he does,' she said flatly, 'and I can prove it. But I didn't even know the house had been sold until I got home, just a few days before he took off on his round-the-world voyage. And it was only after he'd left that I remembered the cache and something that was very precious to me in it.'

'Why the hell didn't you just say so?' Luke Kirwan demanded.

'I would have, if I could have got here *first*—to make sure no one got to it before I did.'

'What was this precious something?' he asked with a frown. 'A heroin haul or the crown jewels?'

'Very funny, Mr Kirwan.' She eyed him sardonically.

'No, but precious enough to me. And when I couldn't get past your secretary, not to mention being treated as if I were a piece of rubbish even after telling her who I was; and when I could never find you home, I remembered I still had a laundry key, and I decided to take matters into my own hands. Don't you think you might have done the same?' she asked gently.

He blinked. 'So—you didn't use the front door?'

'I didn't have a front door key,' she said simply. 'I'd left all my other keys with my father. As a teenager, the laundry door was my—' she grimaced '—preferred way of coming home when I was late.'

He was silent for a long moment, watching her narrowly. Then he said abruptly, 'Did you know I was supposed to be away that night?'

Aurora took her time. This was the tricky bit because if she didn't tread carefully, she could involve Bunny. She frowned at him. 'Were you? What a pity you weren't. I *was* kicking myself for not taking into consideration that you had to be an extraordinarily light sleeper. I swear I didn't make a sound and, believe me, I've had a bit of practice at it, but...' She shrugged.

'You didn't make a sound,' he said slowly. 'And I came home early because I was ill. I got up to go downstairs to find an aspirin or something when I saw this strange light at the bottom of the stairs.'

Aurora smiled suddenly. 'I haven't had much luck, have I?'

He considered, then gestured with his forefinger. 'There's still something that doesn't quite gel, Aurora Templeton. What was it you thought you left behind in that cache that was so precious you couldn't tell anyone about it? I really think I need to see it,' he said pensively, 'before I can believe this story.'

'You can't because it—they—weren't there after all. My diaries,' she said simply.

'Your...*diaries*?'

She nodded. 'My innermost thoughts and secrets that I would hate any strange, prying eyes to see.'

He took a long moment to think around this, then said with a frown, 'If they're not there now, what's happened to them?'

'I think my father must have removed them,' she replied. 'Like any conscientious parent, he probably went through a stage of wondering whether I was on drugs or whatever. I did go through a slightly wild stage,' she confided, 'although certainly not that wild. But I'm now faced with the lowering thought that he probably knew about the cache all along. And my guess is that he packed the diaries up and forgot to tell me.' She sighed ruefully. 'We had so little time together and he was so excited before he left. He's sailing round the world single-handed. I don't know if you knew?'

'I didn't deal with him personally. Can you check it out with him?'

'Yes. He's got a satellite telephone on the boat.'

'So that explains that,' he said slowly. 'You must have confided some pretty intimate thoughts to your diaries to be so paranoid about getting them back unseen by other eyes?'

The slightest tinge of pink entered Aurora's smooth cheeks. 'Would you like any old stranger reading your diaries?' she countered, however.

'I don't keep one, so I don't know,' he replied with the glimmer of a smile. 'What do you do for a living, Miss Templeton?'

She told him, adding, 'I also have an afternoon music programme that I compere three times a week. In between times I volunteer my time as a radio operator for the local Coastguard Association. I'm really quite respectable.'

'So you say,' he commented. 'But, seeing I don't know you from a bar of soap and neither does anyone else, apparently, just how did you get into this party?' he enquired.

'I came with Neil Baker—he's my programme director

and a friend of yours, apparently. It, at the time,' she confessed with a glint of mischief in her eyes, 'seemed like divine intervention, when he invited me because he'd broken up with his girlfriend—and I told you the rest of it.'

'Ah, Neil,' he murmured, 'yes, he is a friend.' But he continued to study her thoughtfully and in a slightly nerve-racking way.

'Does that set your mind to rest about me, Mr Kirwan?' she asked. 'Look, I apologize. The whole thing was rash and misguided—I'm a little prone to that kind of thing but, I can assure you, your secretary did brush me off like a troublesome if not to say somehow shameful fly; I did leave messages for you that you never responded to and I did call to see you at least five times but you were never home.'

'I've been out west a lot lately. So—' he shrugged '—what would you like to do now, Miss Templeton? Go back to the party?'

He took Aurora by surprise. 'Is that all you've got to say?' she asked incredulously.

He eyed her. 'What more is there to say?'

'You could at least apologize for putting me in this awkward position in the first place!'

'Putting you in an awkward position,' he marvelled, his dark eyes suddenly full of wicked amusement. 'You may not recall this, but I did get bitten, scratched and finally knocked out in our first encounter, not to mention made to look a fool.'

'I did not bite you!' Aurora denied hotly. 'Nor did I scratch you—I had gloves on and you must have knocked *yourself* out.'

He raised a quizzical eyebrow. 'Nevertheless, it was like having an angry kitten, spitting and clawing in my arms. Well,' he amended, 'after the first impact of a slim, rather gorgeous little body and, of course—that *unique*, haunting perfume.'

This time his dark gaze was pointedly intimate again as

it stripped away her outfit and dwelt on the curves of her figure beneath it—any doubts she might have had that he was mentally undressing her were embarrassingly laid to rest by the way her body responded to his scrutiny. She could feel herself growing hot and bothered and more than aware of her fluttering pulses.

'I think I'll go home now,' she said unevenly. 'You didn't happen to notice whether Neil had surfaced, by any chance? Not that I need him—' She stopped frustratedly.

'I saw no sign of Neil.'

She shrugged. 'Doesn't matter, I can get a cab.' She picked up her bag.

'Why don't you stay?' he suggested. 'It's only eleven o'clock. I'm sure the party has a bit of life left in it yet.'

She returned his dark gaze with as much composure as she could muster. 'No. No, thank you—'

'We danced well together,' he said meditatively, then grinned. 'I gather it was a case of mistaken identity, your dancing with me at all?'

'Yes, it was!' She eyed him with a mixture of frustration and annoyance. 'Neil pointed out this man who looked exactly like a bumbling, absent-minded professor to me. It never occurred to me it was *you* he was pointing to.'

'My apologies,' he said gravely. '*I* hesitate to point this out to you, but it's never wise to make snap judgements about people on appearance, although Jack has enough of a sense of humour to see the funny side of it,' he assured her.

'Blow Jack,' she retorted bitterly. 'And I have no intention of dancing with you again, Mr Kirwan, because I'm now in a position to make an *informed* judgement on that subject. This meek air you're assuming is entirely false, you're laughing at me behind it and it doesn't blind me to the fact that you're a wolf in sheep's clothing. You even kissed me without one jot of concern for what my preferences in the matter were!'

He smiled satanically. 'Bravo, Aurora—I like that name,

by the way. Your preferences, incidentally, didn't seem to be so contrary to mine,' he pointed out.

'Oh!' She ground her teeth. 'I'm off!' She picked up her bag and slung it over her shoulder.

'Allow me to call a cab for you.' He reached for the bedside phone and did just that. Then he said, although still looking amused, 'Please don't hold this against me but, just to be on the safe side, I'll come down with you and see you into it.'

'Be my guest,' she spat at him, 'but I'm not a burglar or a groupie!'

'Yes, well—' he sobered, and that tough, dangerous side of him was in evidence for a moment '—be that as it may, as you remarked to me, Miss Templeton, and while you may be neither, you do have slightly strange notions about breaking into people's houses and apportioning the blame.' He strolled to the door and opened it. 'After you.'

And to Aurora's extreme indignation, he escorted her downstairs and out onto the porch, and he handed her into the waiting taxi—he even paid for it. But his parting shot was the most humiliating.

'I would have a little more faith in human nature, if I were you, Aurora. You may find life a little less dangerous— unless that's how you get your kicks?'

She argued the matter out with herself during the short drive home in the cab. She paced up and down her living room for ten intense minutes and even consulted her goldfish on the matter, but nothing could alter the fact that there was no better time to retrieve her diaries than right now, while a noisy, crowded party was still in progress. And nothing could alter her determination not to be bested by Luke Kirwan. With the net result that half an hour later, dressed all in black, she was cautiously making her way down the easement once again.

The party was audible as she approached the house from

the rear. As Luke Kirwan had predicted, it still had plenty of life left in it. But as she flitted through the garden like a soundless shadow, no one accosted her, no one was about. The only problem was, there was absolutely no sign of a green rubbish bag stuffed full of her diaries in the hydrangeas below her old bedroom window.

CHAPTER THREE

'MISS HILLIER, my name is Aurora Templeton,' she said down the phone the next morning, a Saturday. 'I would like to speak to Professor Kirwan and, unless *you'd* like me to come and lie down on the front doorstep and go on a hunger strike, don't you *dare* fob me off!'

'That won't be necessary, Miss Templeton,' Miss Hillier replied smoothly. 'Professor Kirwan thought you might like to lunch with him today. Would twelve-thirty be suitable?'

Aurora ground her teeth as she felt, this time, rather like the fly who'd walked into the spider web. Consequently, she said coolly, 'One o'clock would suit me better.'

'That's fine,' Miss Hillier murmured. 'We'll see you then.'

'OK,' she said as she marched out onto the terrace of her old home at five past one, 'hand them over, Mr Kirwan. My diaries.'

Luke Kirwan didn't rise from the cane chair he was lounging in. There was a table for two set for lunch on the terrace and the pool, just beyond, sparkled invitingly beneath a clear blue sky. There was absolutely no sign of a party having been held the night before.

And he summed Aurora up comprehensively, from her tied-back hair, her yellow blouse and white shorts down to her yellow canvas shoes before he said lazily, 'Good afternoon, Aurora. Isn't it a beautiful day? By the way, I was wondering about your legs, but they too are quite stunning.' His gaze returned to them thoughtfully.

Aurora clenched her fists, then swallowed several times

to calm herself and negate the effect of his gaze on her legs. 'I didn't come here to make chit-chat,' she stated.

He lifted his eyes to hers and they were amused, but with a glint of irony as a tinge of pink coloured her cheeks at the same time. 'Why don't you sit down and have a glass of wine instead?' he suggested. 'It might be just what you need after a sleepless night.' He raised his glass to her.

'How did you know—?' She bit her lip.

'You look a little peaked,' he drawled, and got to his feet at last to pull out a chair for her. In blue jeans and a grey T-shirt, he looked casual but big and very fit.

Aurora hesitated, then sank down into it. She also took the glass of wine he poured for her, although absently. 'How did you know,' she began again, 'that I'd dropped them out of the window? I assume that is what happened?'

'You assume correctly.' He sat down. 'I just thought,' he mused, 'that I should take some precautions. It was, after all, only your word I had to go on last night. So I stopped and asked myself what I would have done with anything I had come by—shall we say illegally?'

'There was nothing illegal about it at all! At least by now you must know that.'

'I certainly do.' His gaze was so amused as it rested on her, she flinched visibly. 'But at the time, with Neil having done a bunk—'

'I told you why!' she interrupted fiercely.

'Yes,' he murmured gently. 'Once again I must point out I had no way of knowing if you were telling me the truth.'

Aurora suddenly took a large swallow of wine as some intuition told her that she was in for a battle of wits on a scale she'd never encountered before. 'Now we've sorted it out, though—OK, I concede it was *all* my fault and offer my sincere apologies—could I have my diaries back, please?'

He studied his wine, then raised his dark eyes to her. 'Did

you come straight back to crawl amongst the hydrangeas last night?'

'Uh…no. I spent at least half an hour trying to persuade myself I was…mad.'

'Just as well, we could have bumped into each other—and look what happened the last time we—er—bumped into each other,' he said humorously. 'How often do you have these kind of losing battles with yourself, Aurora?'

She looked at him steadily and refused to reply.

'OK—another tack,' he said wryly. 'What made you unable to persuade yourself you *were* mad?'

She tightened her fingers around the base of her glass as she also attempted to stem the flow of the truth from her lips, but found herself unequal to the task. 'A thorough desire not to be outwitted by a man such as yourself, Mr Kirwan,' she said coldly. 'I don't happen to approve of you in the slightest!'

He laughed softly. 'Because you decided I was on the prowl?'

'Yes,' she said.

'That is unequivocal!' He narrowed his eyes and studied the set of her chin and the warring light in her green eyes until a slight smile twisted his lips. 'There wouldn't also be a slight sense of pique at allowing yourself to—contemplate the pleasures of being led down the garden path by someone as unacceptable as myself?' he queried.

'When did I do that?' Aurora responded, then clicked her tongue. 'OK, but you were to blame for that. I didn't ask you to dance with me and I certainly didn't ask to be kissed!'

'No,' he mused, 'nor could you be held to blame for deliberately deceiving me—about your plans to invade my home again, I mean—since it wasn't me you thought you were dancing with.'

A slight chill ran down Aurora's spine, but Miss Hillier intervened at this point. She wheeled a trolley onto the terrace and invited them to help themselves to lunch.

A few minutes later Aurora was staring at a plate of cold meat and salad in front of her. She picked up her knife and fork, then put them down. 'Have you read them?' she said, her green eyes direct and cold.

'Your diaries? I've glanced through them. For substantiation of your story purposes—who would not have?'

She flinched inwardly but said witheringly, 'So much for trusting human nature! What...' she paused '...do I have to do to get them back? I should warn you to think carefully, Mr Kirwan, before you reply. You've mentioned the police to me. I'm perfectly capable of going to them and reporting blackmail.'

He grinned. 'I see we understand each other, Aurora. However, the police still have an open file on you.'

She gasped. 'You are going to blackmail me!'

He shrugged. 'I just thought it might be a little awkward for someone with as public a profile as you have even to be mentioned in terms of home invasions. I listened to one of your news broadcasts this morning, incidentally. You have a lovely voice on the radio.'

'Before—' Aurora controlled her voice rigidly as she ignored the compliment '—you tell me what it is you require in exchange for my diaries, Mr Kirwan, may I tell you you're wasting your time? Nothing would induce me to sleep with you, my diaries included. If you're that desperate why don't you call on your army of groupies?' she concluded with genuine scorn.

'You've jumped the gun once again, Aurora. I certainly don't expect you to sleep with me immediately.' He helped himself to a crusty brown roll and a pat of yellow butter. 'Although, you must admit you weren't that averse to kissing me.'

'Forget about that,' she ordered, causing him to look wry. 'What did you have in mind?'

'Getting to know you better,' he said lazily.

'Oh, come on! You must think I came down with the last

shower! To all intents and purposes, you're literally rolling in women—' She stopped as he laughed, and she blushed.

But she soldiered on almost immediately. 'Don't forget you yourself told me about the groupies! And I've since remembered Neil mentioning a girl called Leonie something or other—he even thought last night's party might be a surprise engagement party. What are you, Mr Kirwan? A sex maniac?'

But if anything, Luke Kirwan, as he placidly ate his lunch, was even more amused. 'No,' he said at last. 'Although I don't usually kiss girls without some kind of an interest in sleeping with them.'

Aurora's mouth fell open and she stared at him incredulously.

'Why don't you eat your lunch?' he advised, and continued, with lazy irony, 'I would have thought that was human nature. But if I were a sex maniac, do you think I'd go to the lengths I do to protect myself from an army of groupies—as you put it?' He took a leisurely sip of wine. 'After all, you yourself fell foul of those measures.'

Aurora started to eat after another long moment of incredulity, but only because she couldn't think of a thing to come up with to contradict this. Then she had a thought. 'What about Leonie whatever-her-name-is?'

'She need not concern you,' he said serenely.

'You're wrong. None of this concerns me, so let's have no more—nonsense!' Aurora said briskly.

'Very well. What would you like to talk about?'

'Nothing. I just want my diaries back!'

'Then I'm sorry but there's nothing left for me to do until you finish your lunch but—enjoy the view.' He put his knife and fork together; his plate was as clean as a whistle whereas she had hardly made any inroads into her meal.

She ate silently for a while, then said intensely, 'If my father were here, you'd never get away with this!'

'No,' he agreed.

'How can you sit there and admit you're a bastard?'

'I wouldn't go that far.' He raised his eyebrows ruefully. 'Nor have you heard my proposal. It's actually quite honourable.'

Aurora pushed her plate away, her meal unfinished, and looked heavenwards. 'OK, hit me with it. Then I'll tell you exactly what I think of it.'

'In exchange for allowing us to get to know each other better, I'll return one diary per date you have with me. Incidentally, I only intend to keep the last five, that's the last five years so our...agreement would extend for five dates. After that, who knows? The rest you can have back now.'

'And if I don't agree to this?'

He shrugged. 'I guess I'll get to know you through your diaries.'

Aurora's mind worked furiously.

'Don't,' he said softly.

'What?'

'Concoct any more schemes to burgle me.'

She chewed her lip as she gazed at him, trying desperately to come to grips with not only the situation but the man himself.

At last she said abruptly, 'There's got to be more to this. I mean, if you really expect me to believe that your proposal is honourable in any way at all. It's still blackmail, and as for the ''getting to know me'' line—' she shot him a sparkling green look tinged with satire '—there's another line that I'm all too familiar with—men will be men.'

'Go on.' He looked at her attentively.

'How about this—for every girl with a curve, there are several men with an angle. Your angle has got to be quite original, Professor Kirwan, but it doesn't blind me one bit!'

He grinned. 'Anyone would think you'd swallowed a phrase book, Aurora. Got any more?'

'No.' She paused and frowned heavily, then said slowly,

'I still don't see. I mean, I may have attempted to burgle you and outwit you, I certainly don't *like* you, however you may have induced me to kiss you and dance with you— believe me,' she said candidly, 'all the rest of it has well and truly wiped that out! So, unless you have a monumental ego, there's got to be something else behind it.'

She paused again, then looked at him sharply. 'Tell me more about this Leonie person?'

'This Leonie person,' he repeated and grinned. 'I'm only glad she's not here to hear herself referred to thus. Her name is Murdoch, by the way. Uh…we had a relationship, we no longer have a relationship, that's all.'

'How long?'

He shrugged. 'Three years.'

'Oh, yes? And you broke up recently?' Aurora enquired.

'Fairly recently.'

'As in a week or two ago?'

He didn't respond but he didn't look the slightest bit dis-comfited either.

'So either you're on the rebound or looking to show Ms Murdoch a thing or two,' she mused aloud. 'We already know you're on the prowl so…I guess that makes more sense as to why.'

He said nothing.

'I still think it's despicable. Surely you should be old enough to be above playing games with women?' She gazed at him severely.

A smile tugged at his lips, but he replied gravely, 'Perhaps you got it right first time—men will be men. You're very attractive, you know,' he added.

Aurora thought back over the last five years of her life. And for a second it trembled on her lips to tell him he was welcome to keep her diaries and read every word. But a sinking feeling in the pit of her stomach told her she just couldn't do it. It would be like handing her heart and soul to him, although who was to say she could trust him not to read them anyway?

'By the way,' he murmured, 'I packed and sealed the five relevant diaries separately and they're in my safe where no one can get to them, not even Miss Hillier.'

'If that's supposed to reassure, it doesn't, not on any front,' Aurora said cynically.

'You'll just have to trust me.'

She muttered something derogatory and gazed at him broodingly.

'Miss Hillier has made a Mississippi mud cake to die for,' he continued. 'Should we proceed to the coffee and dessert stage since you don't appear to be interested in finishing that?' He gestured towards her plate.

'For a secretary, she's a most amazing all-rounder,' Aurora commented dryly.

'She is. I don't know what I'd do without her.' He rose, collected their plates and took them indoors. Five minutes later, he returned with a tray of coffee and cake. The Mississippi mud cake looked superb in its coating of glistening, smooth dark chocolate with some crystallized violets grouped in the centre, and there was a bowl of whipped cream to go with it. The coffee, in a plunger pot, also smelt divine.

Luke Kirwan cut the cake, placed a large portion in front of Aurora and courteously passed the cream. Then he poured the coffee.

Aurora picked up a cake fork and, with it poised, said, 'What did you have in mind for our first date? Not that I'm agreeing to anything yet and I wouldn't call it a date either— my role of being a stopgap until I bore you rigid, too, because you're jaded, disillusioned or whatever. I think that's a more accurate summing-up of the situation, don't you?'

He merely said, 'Dinner this Wednesday.'

She ate a bite of cake—it *was* superb—and licked some chocolate from her fingertip, then demolished her slice of chocolate heaven and looked longingly at the mud cake. Luke responded with a grin and cut her another slice. 'Just—dinner?' she asked cautiously.

'Aurora,' he murmured, 'despite your protestations to the contrary, I think we may have already crossed a certain divide between a man and a woman. Perhaps it's different for women, but men don't generally fantasize about gorgeous, shapely little bodies without their clothes if they're feeling platonic.' And he allowed that dark gaze to drift over her in a way she remembered all too well.

Causing her to miss her mouth with the cake fork and end up with a blob of chocolate on her upper lip. She muttered a curse and snatched the napkin he offered her. Then she pushed her plate away determinedly, reached for her coffee-cup and tried desperately to banish the memories of being kissed by Luke Kirwan and how her body had felt in his arms.

'But on Wednesday—dinner will do,' he drawled.

She stared at her cup, then looked at him seriously and silently.

'If you didn't enjoy dancing with me, you certainly gave a good imitation of a girl who was revelling in subjecting me to all her feminine powers and wiles,' he said softly.

She swallowed and knew she couldn't deny it. Even the memory was making her feel restless in that special way only a special man could make you feel.

'And you didn't take the opportunity to bite me when I kissed you.'

His words fell into the continuing pool of silence but, although Aurora couldn't tear her gaze away from him, although she could feel herself blushing, a desperate sense of needing to retaliate against this man before she was swamped by those memories started to grow. He might have made her feel uniquely feminine, he might have kissed her more pleasurably than any man ever had, but he was still blackmailing her. And if she wanted her diaries back she was going to have to fight for them, obviously, but also fight not to fall under his spell...

She looked away at last. 'Where?'

'RQ,' he said. 'They have a nice dining room.'

RQ, as she well knew, was affectionate shorthand for the Royal Queensland Yacht Squadron based at Manly, and they did have a nice dining room. 'Are you a member?'

He shook his head. 'But my brother is. He and his wife are up from the country for a couple of weeks of cruising on the bay—they will also be there on Wednesday night.'

Aurora put her head to one side and thought for a bit. To discover there was something else running through her mind, something to do with evening the score between them or—perhaps even a desire to prove to this enigmatic, at times infuriating man that, on a level playing field, she was well able to hold her own.

As in being quite capable of dealing with the dangerously attractive side of him, as in having her feet quite firmly planted on the ground and not being susceptible to being toyed with? she wondered. Was that what she was contemplating? Surely not, yet...

She shrugged. 'I suppose I can't get into too much trouble on the venerable RQ premises or in front of the family, although that's a bit of a surprise—OK.'

'I don't know why I'm not damned with faint praise into thanking you humbly for such magnanimity,' he said wryly.

Aurora smiled coolly for what seemed like the first time for a long time. 'I'll tell you why—humble and Professor Luke Kirwan is a contradiction in terms, that's why.'

'Do you really think so?'

'I know so,' Aurora said. She stood up. 'Thank you for lunch. And I would advise you that, although I've decided to have dinner with you on Wednesday, don't...' She paused and sought the right words.

'Don't get any ideas?' he suggested.

'Exactly.'

He stood up himself and strolled towards her. She didn't move but her eyes widened, then narrowed.

'Relax,' he murmured. 'I'm not going to lay a finger on you. But I think it would be a good idea to allow our dates to follow our—natural inclinations, Aurora.' His gaze slipped up and down her body.

She swallowed uncertainly and trembled visibly, causing an absent smile to cross his lips.

'You might,' she said huskily at last, 'but I have no doubt I'm dealing with someone who could not be termed a gentleman.'

The smile grew. 'Just think how much more exciting it could be, though, especially for someone into fun and adventure as you are, Aurora.'

She licked her lips as her pulses leapt because she had no doubt that being with Luke Kirwan could be all those things—then reminded herself that it would also be a bit like sleeping with the devil. She was going to need a long spoon as it was, she thought chaotically. And did the only thing she was capable of—turned on her heel and walked away.

'Just a moment, Aurora,' he said. 'Don't forget these.' From behind a large pottery urn that held a ficus tree, he produced a green rubbish bag. 'I'm sure you'd like to count them, if nothing else.'

She set her teeth, then walked regally back to him where she accepted the bag from him. 'Do I actually have to count them?'

'No. You can trust me on that too.'

'Personally, I don't think I can trust you any further than I can throw you!'

'But you'll have dinner with me on Wednesday night?' he queried gravely.

'Not from choice, Prof,' she said. 'Not from choice. Would you like to name a time?'

He did so and added that he would pick her up, so she gave him her address and, this time, succeeded in leaving in as dignified a manner as it was possible to at the same time as toting a bulky green rubbish bag—and quite sure her tormentor was laughing at her silently.

'Enjoy the party on Friday? I'm really sorry I abandoned you,' Neil Baker said to Aurora on Monday morning, when their shift ended.

They were drinking tea. It was a cool, wet morning and Aurora wrapped her hands around her mug. 'It certainly was a lively party,' she commented neutrally, then grinned a little wickedly. 'Did you and your girlfriend make up or did things get worse?'

Neil sighed. 'We are back together but I don't know for how long. Mandy is...it's a case of can't live together, can't live apart.' He gazed at his mug. 'Oh, well, we'll see. What did you think of Luke?'

Aurora shrugged. 'Quite impressive and not what you'd expect. He doesn't look particularly scholarly.' She heard the dry note in her voice.

But Neil appeared to miss it as he replied enthusiastically, 'That's the beauty of Luke. You'd expect him to be dry and desiccated, but he surely isn't.'

'So I gather. Tell me about this Leonie Murdoch? You mentioned you thought Friday night's bash might have been an engagement party?'

'Ah.' Neil looked rueful. 'I was a bit out of date there, apparently. Mandy knows Leonie and it would appear that they've broken up just when everyone thought they were getting engaged—two days before the party, in fact; the party was more Leonie's idea than his, apparently, then it was too late to cancel. He needs his head read. Mandy sides with Leonie, of course—girls sticking together, kind of thing—and puts all the blame on Luke, but in this case I have to agree. Leonie Murdoch is a ten! If not to say an eleven or twelve!'

Aurora blinked. 'That gorgeous, et cetera, et cetera?'

'In a word, yes. She's also very bright and brainy, she's a stockbroker.'

'So,' Aurora said slowly, 'she's upset about the break-up?'

'Well, she's putting on a brave face, but Mandy reckons she's devastated underneath. Luke…' Neil paused '…has always had women running after him. So the concept of monogamy could be a little foreign to him.'

'You don't say!' Aurora's expression was full of disdain.

'Why—' Neil focused intently on her suddenly '—do I get the feeling you didn't like him?'

'I…it's a long story, but men who are God's gift to women bore me silly.'

'I don't think he gets around like that!' Neil protested.

'You're not a woman,' Aurora pointed out. 'And you're the one who mentioned monogamy.'

'Yes, but…' he paused and frowned '…what exactly happened between you two?'

'Nothing much,' Aurora replied airily, then subsided. 'But I'm having dinner with him on Wednesday and I'm not sure—I'm even less sure now that it's a good idea.'

Neil stared at her, then blinked twice, but appeared to be bereft of speech.

'You're comparing me with Leonie Murdoch and finding me wanting?' Aurora suggested.

'I…well, no…I mean—'

'Don't lie, Neil,' Aurora said with a gurgle of laughter. 'I could see the circles of your mind spinning in your eyes. She *must* be quite something because, although I'm not a stockbroker or a ''ten'', I don't have two heads or anything like that, do I?'

'No, no. Of course not. No,' he insisted. 'In fact, you're something else yourself, Aurora. Enough to make Mandy absolutely furious with jealousy, as it happened, but—'

'Not quite in their league? The Luke Kirwans and Leonie

Murdochs of this world?' Aurora suggested, still smiling as she posed the question. 'Well, we'll see.'

'Aurora,' Neil said a shade apprehensively, 'don't let anything I said...I mean, I shouldn't have...I was only theorizing...' He stopped helplessly.

'Don't worry, Neil, I won't,' she promised, with her eyes very green and very bright—something that would have put the fear of God into Bunny and her father, and didn't, as it happened, reassure Neil Baker much either.

Luke Kirwan was early when he came to pick her up on Wednesday, but she wasn't even changed when he knocked on the door of her town house.

'I'm sorry,' she said as she opened the door, 'but there's been a bit of a kerfuffle at the Coastguard. A yacht stranded on a sand bank on the South Passage Bar. So my shift went overtime because the person due to take over from me went out on the rescue boat.'

'Oh.' He looked her up and down in her white boiler suit with the Coastguard logo and studied her thick plait. 'Are they all right?'

'Yep. They got them towed off safely, but there was a woman aboard having hysterics, which didn't help.'

He smiled. 'You don't approve, I gather?'

She shrugged. 'It was pretty scary stuff. But I just don't think you should be out on boats if you don't think you can cope with emergencies.'

'Do you do any of the actual rescue work yourself?' he asked.

'No. I'm just a radio operator. Look, come in and help yourself to a drink.' She led the way into the lounge and pointed to an open cocktail cabinet. 'I promise you I'll be fifteen minutes at the most!'

'You don't have to rush. If I can use the phone, I can ring the club and leave a message to say we'll be a bit late.'

'I like rushing,' Aurora said. 'With plenty of time to get

dressed I can change my mind about what to wear at least half a dozen times and still end up unhappy with my choice.'

'Oh.' His lips twisted. 'Then please do rush, Aurora. I wouldn't like to see you unhappy.'

It took her five minutes to shower, five minutes to dress and the last five to apply a minimum of make-up and brush out her hair. Despite all this activity, she reminded herself of how she'd decided to play this evening. Quite normal, friendly even, but definitely not susceptible to any satanic overtures from Luke Kirwan. She grabbed her bag, shoes and a scarf in passing.

'There,' she said to him as she arrived back in the lounge. 'Is that a demonstration of power dressing, sheer masterful organization—or what?' She slipped on her shoes and raised her hands to gather her hair and comb it with her fingers, preparatory to tying it back with the scarf.

He was sitting in the winged armchair but he stood up and put his hands into the pockets of his fawn trousers, worn with a beautiful blue linen shirt. And he took in her emerald chiffon blouse with its stiff collar and cuffs, her sleek long black skirt with a slit up the thigh to reveal sheer black stockings, and high black heels. Her scarf matched the blouse and her bag was embroidered with black, gold and emerald beads.

'Not only that, but I think the result is masterful too, although beautiful would be a better way to describe it,' he said finally.

Aurora lowered her arms, conscious suddenly of the way her breasts were outlined beneath the chiffon, and shrugged. 'So long as I don't disgrace you in front of your brother and his wife, not to mention RQ! Shall we go? Oh, didn't you want a drink?'

He paused and held her gaze in a way that made her aware that her slight confusion to do with the outline of her body being on parade beneath his dark eyes was all too apparent to him. And it wasn't until she'd turned faintly pink that he said politely, 'Thank you, but no. I thought I'd wait.' He looked around. 'I've been talking to your fish.'

Aurora grinned. She had a small, colourfully embellished tank but only two goldfish so far in it. 'One of the good things about Annie and Ralph is that they don't talk back to you. I could swear from their expressions that they do listen, though.'

'Their expressions actually change?' he asked quizzically.

'Once you get to know them, yes, certainly. I thought of getting a bird, but I really feel sorry for birds in cages, so fish seemed to be a good alternative.' A glint of mischief lit her green eyes. 'Better than talking to yourself, surely?'

'What about your diaries?'

'Well, now.' She shrugged and wondered if this was his unsubtle way of reminding her about the hold he had over her. 'I've been a little circumspect there lately. Thanks to you. But I'm sure I'll get back into it.'

'I hope you do. I'd hate to be responsible for curtailing your creative genius.' His lips twisted at her dark expression and he said then, obviously changing the subject, 'Do you feel claustrophobic at all, living here after the house?'

Aurora, still smarting from the fact that he'd had the nerve to mention her diaries but determined not to show it, launched into a random speech. 'I haven't really had the time for any claustrophobia to kick in. But as town houses go, it's nice, isn't it? I know it's a bit cluttered at the moment—I've got all the treasures from the house that Dad couldn't bear to part with. Of course, he had to part with a lot, which actually annoyed me somewhat but—' She stopped and grimaced. 'Don't let me ramble on! Oh, by the way, since you brought the subject up, perhaps I should give you this.'

This was a key that she picked up from the bureau. He took it and studied it as it lay in the palm of his hand. Then he raised his dark eyes to hers. 'The spare laundry key, I take it?'

'Yes.'

'I'd forgotten about it,' he said with a faint smile and a teasing little look.

She raised her eyebrows ironically. 'I hadn't.'

'Thank you.' He slipped it into his pocket. 'So you have no further plans to burgle me, Aurora?'

'Obviously not. And I certainly don't plan to be a suspect because I have a key to the house in my possession should you ever really be burgled.'

'I see,' he said thoughtfully. 'I gather I'm not forgiven, then?'

She bit her lip. It hadn't been part of her plan to let him know she wasn't going to be a willing victim to his black-mail scheme, but she could see this might be easier said than done. If only he hadn't mentioned her damn diaries on top of making her feel edgy in a very physical way! So how to regroup?

She didn't; she made things worse if anything, but couldn't help herself. 'If you didn't…somehow keep making me feel as if you'd like to…' She stopped frustratedly.

'I'd like to go to bed with you?' he suggested mildly.

'Yes!' Her green eyes were fierce and her fists clenched. 'Believe me, I have no intention of allowing that to happen.'

'Then should we go to dinner instead?' He consulted his watch. 'It is getting late now.'

'Is that all you've got to say?' she demanded.

'You've used that line before,' he reminded her.

Aurora turned away, ground her teeth, then picked up her bag and marched to the door. He followed her, shrugging into his tweed jacket, and waited while she locked the door behind them. She dropped the keys into her bag but when she glanced at him through her lashes it was to disturb such a look of humorous appreciation in his eyes, she was flooded with all sorts of sensations. But the chief ones were to feel disconcerted instead of annoyed—and rather young.

CHAPTER FOUR

'I MIGHT have known,' Aurora said as she slid into the front seat of his yellow, convertible Saab.

Luke Kirwan glinted an unspoken question at her.

'That your car would be in keeping with everything else that is so misleading about you,' she elucidated. 'Mind you, it's very nice, trendy and yuppie, et cetera.'

He said ruefully as he drove off, 'Is that how you see me—trendy and yuppie?'

Aurora shrugged. 'Scholarly was the last thing that entered my mind when I saw you, as we both know.'

'What about nice?'

'No, nice didn't occur to me at the time either,' she conceded, 'and, to be honest, neither did yuppie.'

'So what did occur to you, Aurora?' he queried as he turned into the RQ car park.

She considered briefly. 'I'd rather not say at the moment.'

'Is this going to be a test like sweaty palms and treading on your toes?'

She tilted her chin and favoured him with an enigmatic green gaze. 'Perhaps.'

He laughed softly, then said, 'As a matter of fact, this car appeals to the engineer in me, that's why I drive it.'

'I might have believed that if you'd gone for a black one,' she said gravely. 'But yellow? Surely that has to be a statement of some kind?'

'What colour car do you drive?' he countered.

'A sort of pearly watermelon pink,' she said demurely. 'But then I'm not a professor of anything.' She shrugged. 'I'm also a girl and expected to be colourful.'

He pulled the yellow Saab up in a parking slot and

switched off the engine. 'So you are—colourful,' he remarked. 'OK, I fully intended to get a neutral colour only to find I couldn't resist this one. I don't know what hidden facets of my character this indicates, but it gives me a deep sense of satisfaction to be seen driving this car and this colour.'

'See?' Aurora smiled sunnily at him. 'It's quite easy to be honest when one really sets one's mind to it. And I don't hold the colour of your car against you at all, so long as you're honest about it.'

'I'll store that piece of information away for future reference,' he said a little dryly. 'Nor is it the time and place to go into the fact that I haven't been intentionally dishonest with you—'

'It isn't,' Aurora broke in to agree. 'We're definitely late now, Mr Kirwan. Not only that, I'm starving!'

But although he opened his door and the overhead light came on, it was a long moment before he got out. And it was a curiously heavy-lidded gaze he subjected her to that set her skin tingling just when she'd been congratulating herself that she'd got the reins back in her hands, so to speak. The reins of not falling for the dangerously attractive side of Luke Kirwan as well as playing her own game.

He said nothing, however, then he did get out, leaving her feeling shaken and not at all sure—of anything.

Barry Kirwan and his wife, Julia, were already seated and waiting for them.

Barry was in his early thirties, as tall as his brother but sandy-haired and playful. And Julia Kirwan was one of those down-to-earth, straight-talking girls, although attractive with big blue eyes and a very short cap of fine, fair hair.

But it was obvious they both felt slightly awkward at first, as if trying to assess how serious Leonie Murdoch's replacement might be in Luke Kirwan's scheme of things. When one of Aurora's coastguard colleagues came over to the table and congratulated her on the way she'd handled the afternoon's drama, the ice was broken immediately, though.

'Was that you on the radio this afternoon?' Barry said incredulously. 'We were out on the bay at the time and we listened to it all—you were fantastic!' he said enthusiastically. 'Especially the way you calmed that poor woman down.'

'Thank you,' Aurora responded, and the evening perked up considerably as they talked boats and boating, and sheep stations—Barry managed two of the family properties—and Aurora's career as a radio broadcaster.

Then Julia suggested they visit the powder room and Aurora had been enjoying herself so much, she didn't stop to think about what she might be letting herself in for...

They were touching up their make-up side by side when Julia looked at her in the mirror and said straightly, 'Do you know about Leonie, Aurora?'

Aurora capped her lipstick and ran a finger around the outline of her mouth. 'Yes, as a matter of fact, although I've never met her.'

'We all thought Luke bought his new house because they were getting married.'

'So I believe,' Aurora murmured, not looking back at Julia in the mirror.

'I just thought I ought to warn you,' Julia went on, 'that he could be in a...dangerous frame of mind.'

Aurora's lashes lifted and their gazes locked in the mirror. 'In what way?'

Julia shrugged. 'In the way that if he still wants Leonie, but on his terms, say, then he might, well...use someone to make her jealous.'

'What different kind of terms could he have in mind other than marrying her?' Aurora asked.

'Perhaps he wanted her to give up her career to fit in with his own. Look—' Julia hesitated, then went on frustratedly '—it's just that they were such a great couple, no one can believe this has happened. So I...perhaps I shouldn't have but, anyway, I felt conscience-bound to say something.'

'Thank you, Julia,' Aurora said, although she was actually thinking that in different circumstances she might have found the other girl's candour more like a natural talent for meddling. 'But I'm not serious about Luke so you don't need to worry.'

Julia turned from the mirror for the first time and regarded Aurora directly. 'It wouldn't be hard to join a long line of women who thought the same,' she observed.

You, too, before you married his brother? it crossed Aurora's mind to think from nowhere—but she was just on the verge of dismissing the thought as being uncharitable, if nothing else, when Julia turned away as a faint pink began to creep up her neck.

Aurora blinked, then popped her lipstick into her bag at the same time as she thought, Glory be! Luke Kirwan had a lot to answer for. But all the better, really. All the more ammunition to add to her arsenal...

The evening broke up not long after that.

It was eleven-thirty and Aurora said ruefully, 'Oh! I've got to get up at five tomorrow, I really should be getting home to bed!'

Luke stood up. Of the four of them, he'd probably said the least, Aurora suddenly realized, yet he hadn't looked bored or as if he hadn't been enjoying himself.

But when they'd parted from Barry and Julia, after Barry, at least, had enthusiastically expressed the hope that they'd meet again, and were walking to the car, Luke said, 'That wasn't so bad, was it?'

Aurora grimaced. 'No. In fact I think I did an awful lot of the talking.'

He looked down at her, amusedly.

Aurora stopped walking. 'You were not nearly so loquacious,' she remarked. 'Were you being inwardly superior?'

'Did I look as if I was?'

She considered. 'No. But, now I come to think of it, it was a bit like a test of some kind.'

'Well, you came through with flying colours, but it wasn't.'

'I…so why were you so quiet?' she asked slowly.

It was another overcast night, windy and with ragged clouds pursuing a bright new moon. When the moon evaded the clouds, trees surrounding the car park cast stunted shadows and the wind bore not only a salty smell on the air but the unmistakable jangle of a marina close by as it sped through the shrouds of many a yacht. It also lifted Aurora's hair and fluttered her emerald scarf as she waited for Luke Kirwan to answer.

'I was slightly—preoccupied, I guess you could say,' he replied at last.

'Work?' she hazarded, then looked rueful. 'Groupies? Or—are you sure you weren't measuring my social skills up against Leonie Murdoch's?'

'Perfectly sure. I was wondering what it would be like to kiss you again,' he said, quite casually.

Aurora's immediate reaction was to back away hastily, which brought her up against the yellow Saab, causing Luke Kirwan to smile faintly, and add, 'I don't intend to find out here and now.' He produced the keys and opened the door for her.

It wasn't until they were driving along that she could think of anything to say, and then the words burst out against her better judgement. 'All evening?' she said incredulously.

'On and off.' He shrugged. 'Don't you see yourself as kissable? I would have thought I demonstrated otherwise on Friday night.'

Conscious of the possibility of walking into a trap, she said stiffly after a slight pause, 'That's got nothing to do with it. I—'

'But don't you?' he persisted.

'Of course I do—that's to say, *when* I think about it, which is not—it's not one of my preoccupations…I knew you were going to tie me up in knots!' She looked at him bitterly. 'And thank heaven I didn't know about it at the time!'

He laughed. 'How do you think you might have reacted?'

'I'd have probably been all hot and bothered,' she replied tartly.

'As in filled with revulsion or—wondering how a certain set of circumstances between us has failed to be amenable to your planning?'

'I…I'm not sure…how do you mean?' she asked disjointedly.

He pulled the car up outside her town house, switched off and turned to her. 'Your decision to hold me at arm's length, Aurora, if not to teach me a thing or two at the same time.'

Her eyes widened and her lips parted.

He waited, with grave attention. But when she could only look crestfallen, a wicked little smile twisted his lips. 'I'll see you in.'

'It's OK, I…I'll be fine.'

'I was only intending to walk you to your front door.'

'Gallantry I could live without,' Aurora muttered, then looked embarrassed.

His smile deepened as he got out and came round to open her door.

'Thank you,' she said, attempting to step out regally but catching her heel in the hem of her skirt so that she actually toppled out into his arms.

They closed about her and he picked her up and sat her on the bonnet while he disentangled her heel. He studied her shoe for a moment, then slipped it carefully on her foot at the same time as he murmured, 'What a pity I'm not Prince Charming. This is also coming adrift,' he added, and put his arms around her neck to retie the scarf around her hair. Then he rested one hand on her shoulder and traced the line of her eyebrows delicately with a fingertip. 'There, all present and correct,' he said wryly.

Aurora could still feel his fingers on her foot, the nape of her neck and her eyebrows. For some reason, the way he'd handled her in those places, although with the lightest touch, had left a tingling sensation behind, but not only that. She was uniquely conscious of everything about this tall man who had spent the evening contemplating kissing her.

She breathed in the clean linen fragrance of his shirt tinged with pure man, and thought she'd like to see him without a shirt because she had the strong feeling he was fashioned rather beautifully beneath his clothes. Then there were those eyes, that hawk-like look sometimes and the fascinating hollows beneath his cheekbones; and the way he'd picked her up as if she were as light as thistledown.

But it was also the little things he did and the way she responded to them, she thought, as if being intensely familiar with this man whom she barely knew, who tidied her hair, smoothed her eyebrows and restored her shoe to her foot, was almost second nature to her. How strange, she marvelled. It's as if he knows me better than I know myself, otherwise I'd be resisting and resenting him rather than thinking how nice it is...no, really, Aurora, you need to take a stand!

'I swear,' she responded at last, 'that I am jinxed at times and never more so than in relation to you, Luke Kirwan!'

'I don't know about jinxed,' he replied with a lurking smile. 'It could be that someone up there likes me—since I swore I wouldn't be so obvious as to attempt to kiss you goodnight.'

'Are you going to?' she asked.

'Put it this way, would you like me to, now we're...in such close contact?'

'That's—well, at least that's an improvement,' Aurora commented, more for something to say as she sat on the bonnet, desperately trying to withstand the sheer niceness of being so close to him. 'You didn't give me any choice the last time.'

'Actually, sitting there, especially if I step off the pavement—' he did so '—makes you just the right height for me to kiss comfortably now—another consideration,' he said.

'I'm sorry if I'm not tall enough for you,' she said tartly.

'Strange you should mention that,' he commented gravely. 'I did believe I had a preference for taller girls, but it seems to have flown out of the window lately. You don't contravene my preferences in any other respect, I should add.'

'Oh! That's—'

'Great legs, but I've told you about those; lovely skin; fantastic eyes and a figure to—'

'I think you should stop right there, Professor,' she said ominously. 'I hate the idea of being totted up against a set of preferences!'

'You're welcome to return the compliment,' he replied mildly. 'What do you usually go for in a man? By the way, you were going to tell me what you thought of me on first impressions earlier—not trendy and yuppie, apparently.'

'But not scholarly either, remember?' she said with some irony. 'Uh—a latter-day Mr Darcy—was one of them anyway.'

He laughed softly. 'Proud?'

'Proud, bored, dangerous—I was right.'

'Bored? Perhaps,' he conceded. 'But proud? I don't see where you got that from.'

'You wouldn't.' She studied him darkly. 'It's the last one I'm concerned about at the moment, though. You do happen to have me trapped on the bonnet of your car. Not to mention the rather public aspect of it.'

'Aurora, you're absolutely right. I did think I mightn't be able to help myself—from kissing you. You feel so nice.' He moved his hands down her arms to clasp her waist. 'You smell so nice. And it was a rather memorable experience the last time we did it.' He stopped and looked into her eyes with a little glint of mockery in his own.

Aurora trembled suddenly and was conscious of a crazy desire to say—Just go ahead and do it, Luke, because now I can't get it off *my* mind! But she bit her lip instead.

He smiled crookedly and lifted her down. 'I shall bow to your good sense, however, as well as proving I'm not dangerous at all!' He released her and strolled around to the driver's side. 'Goodnight, Miss Templeton. Sleep well! I'll be in touch some time.' And he slid into the Saab and drove off with a casual wave.

Leaving Aurora on the pavement prey to a veritable Pandora's box of emotions and sensations, one of them being that he was laughing at her... But it was only when she gained the sanctuary of her town house that she gave rein to emotions.

'Who the hell does he think he is?' she asked her goldfish as she stood in the middle of her lounge with her hands on her hips, having flung her bag down on a chair ungently.

But the even more annoying thought, she discovered as she started to pace the room, was her own reaction to him. Talk about behaving like a dewy-eyed schoolgirl, she marvelled, and groaned aloud as she thought of herself stranded on the pavement by a deep sense of disappointment while he drove off waving...

So, how to set the record straight? she pondered. By having nothing further to do with Luke Kirwan, she answered herself severely. Simple as that and for once in your life, Aurora Templeton, *don't* be tempted to redress things or...give back as good as you got!

What about her diaries, though? was her next thought.

The next morning, when she got home from her early news shift, she received an unexpected visitor—Miss Hillier.

'Oh! This is a surprise,' she said when she opened the

door, then her gaze fell on the parcel in Miss Hillier's hands. 'Is that—'

'I don't know exactly what it is,' Miss Hillier said. 'Professor Kirwan asked me to deliver it to you. May I come in for a moment, Aurora?'

'Well, yes.' Aurora led her into the lounge. 'Would you like a cup of tea?'

Miss Hillier sat down. 'No, thank you.'

Aurora hesitated, then sat down opposite, to find herself on the receiving end of an unnerving stare.

She cleared her throat.

Miss Hillier put the parcel down on the table. 'Aurora, although I don't know what this is, and although I do now know you're not what I first thought you to be, I think I should still warn you that you could be playing with fire.'

Aurora chewed her lip, then said tersely, 'What is he really? The devil in disguise?'

Miss Hillier blinked. 'How do you mean?'

'I happen to *know* that he's not exactly a gentleman, but this is the second warning I've had on the subject.'

'He can be a *perfect* gentleman,' Miss Hillier said stiffly, then stopped and sighed. 'But there's obviously some game going on between you two and I can't help knowing…well, that since he broke up with Miss Murdoch he's been… different.'

'I should hope so,' Aurora said, tartly this time. 'Because if the way he's dealing with me is his usual *modus operandi* then he's nothing but a cad, albeit a very attractive one.' She looked ceiling-ward.

'Men,' Miss Hillier said slowly, 'are…can be…difficult.'

Aurora laughed unamusedly.

'But I did believe he was very much in love with Miss Murdoch and to see him, so very soon, attaching the interest of another woman just…it doesn't make sense!' she finished frustratedly.

'It's beginning to make very good sense to me, Miss

Hillier,' Aurora said grimly. 'He's trying to make her jealous.'

Miss Hillier blinked again. 'If you know that, why are you going along with it?'

'I'll tell you.' Aurora reached for the packet, stripped the wrapping and revealed one her diaries. 'You remember that attempted burglary? It was me, trying to get my diaries back.' And she explained it all.

Miss Hillier sat transfixed for a long moment at the end of it, then she said helplessly, 'If only you'd told me…'

'If only I had,' Aurora agreed in a heartfelt way. 'But there's something that makes it impossible for me to…' She stopped and got up to pace around with her arms folded. 'Not only that, but he's holding the police file over my head.'

'Oh, he wouldn't…would he?'

Aurora stopped in front of Miss Hillier. 'You tell me, you know him much better than I do.'

Miss Hillier hesitated. 'He…doesn't like to be crossed,' she said at last.

'I gathered that.' Aurora took a breath. 'You could end this farce, Miss Hillier. You could surely point out to him how…low he's being.'

Luke's secretary stood up. 'I don't—' she started to say, but Aurora interrupted.

'I mean to say, not only you—but his own sister-in-law has warned me about getting my fingers burnt. Personally, I suspect Leonie Murdoch is the one you're more worried about, but on one thing I do agree. I have four more "dates" to endure with Luke Kirwan and I am literally under siege.'

'To…to sleep with him?' Miss Hillier asked dazedly.

Aurora shrugged. 'When he sets his mind to it, he can be dynamite.'

'So you're not entirely unaffected by him?'

Aurora paused. 'Sadly, I didn't know who he was at first and I found him, let's just say, intriguing.'

'I'll do what I can,' Miss Hillier said abruptly. 'But I'm now very worried about him. All this is extremely out of character. He's obviously much more affected by the break-up with Miss Murdoch than I realized.' And she took her leave.

Why do I get the feeling I'm the last person anyone need concern themselves within all this? Aurora asked herself with considerable irony.

She got a response that same evening, just after she'd finished reading her five-year-old diary—a mistake, she had to concede. It was the year she'd fallen passionately in love with a married man, not that he'd ever known about it, but all the impossible and exotic scenarios she'd dreamt up to bring them together were there on the pages in black and white.

'Nice try, Aurora,' Luke said casually down the line when she picked up the phone, 'but Miss Hillier is not subornable.'

'Then she's a disgrace to her sex,' Aurora shot back.

'Oh, I've been given a piece of her mind, all right. But short of burgling my safe herself, there's not much else she can do. Incidentally,' he drawled, 'I gather Julia had a go at you as well?'

'She did. *Incidentally*,' she parodied, 'we're all of the same mind. That you're using me to make your ex, or whatever she is, jealous.'

'You're wrong, you know,' he said lightly. 'The more I see of you, the more I want to get to know you. But there is the other way to do that.'

Aurora looked down at the diary in her lap, and flinched. 'Doesn't it mean anything to you that I have to *despise* you for this?'

'Well, you still haven't slapped me, bitten me or told me to go to hell—in certain circumstances—so I'm not too sure about that. And it's only four to go now—are you seriously afraid that you can't resist me for four more dates?'

Aurora couldn't speak.

He waited a moment, then said merely, 'I'll be in touch.' And put the phone down.

It was three weeks before she heard from him again.

Three uncomfortable weeks during which she felt as if she were on an emotional roller coaster. Mainly because there was one small area of her that could not entirely hate Luke Kirwan, impossible as it seemed.

She composed and rehearsed fiery, cutting speeches. She visualised getting him so besotted with her that he would be devastated when she walked away from him. She also visualised Leonie Murdoch walking away from Luke Kirwan, but as the days passed she lost a lot of her bite. In fact, she even started to feel outraged in the opposite direction...

How could he spend a whole evening wondering about kissing her, then leave her dangling for weeks?

To make matters worse, she was all too aware that the ambivalent state of her mind was responsible for these unreasonable cross currents in her thinking on the subject of a blackmailer.

Then there were Neil's questions to field. He'd been intensely interested in how the dinner had gone, and, perhaps fuelled by Aurora's disinclination to expand upon it, asked her several times if she'd heard any more from Luke.

Or, she paused to think one day, had Neil been recruited by Mandy, on Leonie Murdoch's behalf, to report on the state of play between herself and the professor? His keenness for the subject seemed a bit excessive otherwise.

In a bid to disengage her mind from the topic, Aurora threw herself into properly organizing her new home, and took up gardening. She also spoke to her father a few times. He was having a whale of a time exploring Pacific islands, which she was happy to hear but it was impossible for her to relax. Then it crept into her mind that, despite a busy, fulfilling life, she was lonely and even the company of a blackmailer would be better than none…

She was actually gardening when this thought struck, and she reared back from it physically, as if the rose bush she was planting had plunged its thorns into her flesh. And that was how Luke Kirwan found her when he came to call—kneeling upright on the lawn and staring into space as if she'd been mummified.

In fact he said her name twice before she responded, and the way she responded was to be like a thorn of embarrassment to her for quite some time. She turned, nearly toppled over in surprise and said, spontaneously speaking her mind, 'Oh—go away, please! You've complicated my life enough as it is!'

'I beg your pardon, Aurora?' he drawled.

Of course she blushed scarlet, and when she wiped her face she left a streak of dirt on it. Then she tripped on her trowel as she staggered to her feet and had to suffer the indignity of his helping hand to restore her balance, but not only that—the quizzical set of his eyebrows and the fact that he was trying not to laugh.

Then he said, 'I've come to take you out to lunch, but perhaps you'd like to clean up first?'

In spite of her several causes for deep embarrassment, Aurora was instantly moved to express her own satirical reaction. 'You didn't think you ought to call first? In case I wasn't here or I had something else on, or—I simply might not have wanted to go to lunch with you?'

'Well?' he said mildly. 'Are you any of those things—apart from obviously being here?'

'I…' She gritted her teeth. 'I…need to think about it.' And shrivelled inwardly at such a feeble response.

He didn't laugh. He did say, 'May I come in and have a cup of coffee with you while you do?' Which was as good as laughing at her, she felt, and he added, 'Then we could make a decision about lunch.'

'Would that constitute one date or two?' she asked acidly.

'I might be able to see my way to making it two,' he replied.

She eyed him, then shrugged and turned away. He followed her inside via the front patio and through the lounge to the kitchen where she put the kettle on.

'May I?' he queried.

'May you what?'

'Make the coffee while you have a shower? I'm sure you'll feel better for it.'

Aurora looked down at herself. She wore an old pair of khaki shorts with a once-white T-shirt now yellow with age, her knees were dirty and her feet were bare. 'Can you? Without Miss Hillier to hold your hand?'

'Yep.' He grinned. 'If you have a plunger pot and real coffee.'

Aurora looked heavenwards and produced not only a plunger pot but coffee beans and a grinder. 'There. The only thing you don't have to do is go to Arusha to get it.'

'It so happens I've been to Arusha,' he commented.

'So have I.' Her expression indicated this was no big deal.

'Well, we could swap experiences,' he suggested comfortably.

Aurora studied him—he was in the same jeans and grey T-shirt as on that never-to-be-forgotten lunch occasion at her old home. Not quite the corsair, the better-than-any-of-them James Bond or the Mr Darcy she'd first imagined him as, but not because he was any less physically impressive, just better known to her now. Only, she thought gloomily, that made him all the better—or was it worse?

She shook her head, left the kitchen and went upstairs with no further ado.

This time she took her time. It was half an hour later when she came back down wearing a straight skirt to just above her ankles, taupe cotton with tiny white dots, and a short white sleeveless top. Flat, strappy sandals completed her out-fit and her hair was damp and up in a knot.

Luke Kirwan rose on her arrival, boiled the kettle, poured the water into the plunger pot and brought a tray on which he had assembled cups, milk and sugar and some biscuits into the lounge. What he had occupied himself with while he'd waited was a sports programme on television, she saw.

She sat down opposite the tray, which he'd placed on her unusual coffee table—an elephant bearing a round brass ta-ble-top.

'Feeling better?' he asked.

'Yes, much better, thank you.' She plunged the coffee and poured two cups. He took one and sat down in the winged chair.

'You've—' he looked around '—sorted the chaos. It looks very nice. I take it you and your father did a lot of travelling together?'

'We did. I just wish I was island-hopping with him in the South Pacific at the moment,' Aurora replied, unwisely as it happened.

'That bad?'

She stilled in the act of stirring her coffee and slowly placed the spoon in the saucer, very conscious of the nar-rowed way he was watching her. 'What do you mean?'

'Have I complicated your life to that extent, Aurora?'

'No! Of course not,' she denied. 'I…it's just that…I feel a little flat at the moment. Probably the natural consequence of coming back from a six-month overseas trip myself, that kind of thing.' She flipped a hand casually.

'So what did you mean earlier?' he asked.

She thought for a moment. 'It must be obvious. Until I get all my diaries back, you have complicated my life. Unnecessarily, what's more.' She studied him with her chin lifted, her eyes challenging.

'I…' He paused and raised an eyebrow. 'Unless you sus-pect I'm about to take advantage of you here and now—'

he looked around '—or during what I had in mind for lunch, I don't see what's so…difficult about it all.'

'You wouldn't,' she retorted unwisely.

'Then why don't you explain, Aurora?' he invited.

She took a deep breath, and all the nervous tension she'd endured for the last weeks rose to the top, killing stone-dead any ploys she might have devised for beating Luke Kirwan at his own game. 'Don't think I don't know,' she said intensely, 'what you're up to. You're not going to be satisfied until you have me so besotted I'll willingly go to bed with you!'

An alert gleam entered his dark eyes but he said nothing.

'And I know why,' she continued, past all good sense now. 'Yes, your break-up with Leonie may have a lot to do with it, but the other reason is—you hate the thought of not being able to click your fingers at a girl whenever the whim takes you!'

'It is rather a novelty,' he agreed mildly.

She stared at him.

'You didn't expect me to admit it?'

'I'm just trying to work out if it makes you better or worse—' She stopped abruptly and bit her lip—it was the second time she'd entertained that sentiment in the space of half an hour.

'But the other reason I have, Aurora, is that you never bore me,' he said.

'What…what about Leonie?'

He sat back and stared absently into space. Then his lips twisted into a dry smile. 'I'm amazed at everyone's concern on that score—Leonie and I agreed to come to a parting of the ways.'

'End of story?' Aurora suggested with irony.

'Yep. By the way, my sister-in-law, my secretary and anyone else you may have been taking advice from on the subject—'

'Mandy Pearson, for instance,' Aurora put in.

'Ah, Mandy.' He looked sardonic.

'I haven't *spoken* to her,' Aurora said hastily. 'I wouldn't even have known of the connection if it wasn't for Neil—he was the one who, well, in response to a little fishing I did he...' She shrugged.

'Spilt the beans? Anyway,' Luke said, 'none of them are entitled, or indeed competent, to comment.'

Aurora considered this. 'If all that's true, why do you need to blackmail me?'

'Are you suggesting you'd allow me to continue to get to know you without holding onto your diaries?' He raised a dark eyebrow at her.

Aurora hesitated. 'I see your point,' she said at length and shivered suddenly.

'What?' he queried.

'I don't know if I like you or hate you—I don't know if I could trust you.'

'There's only one way to solve that,' he observed.

'Perhaps—all right,' she said with sudden decision. 'If you consider this two dates, I'll have two more with you. Then, when I get my diaries back, I...might reconsider.'

'You mean reassess your judgement of me?'

'And exactly what your intentions are, Prof,' she said with some acerbity.

'I shall look forward to it—so, you will come to lunch?'

'Yes. Where?'

'Well, since it's such a beautiful day, I thought we might take the fast ferry to Dunwich, then a taxi over to Point Lookout, have a swim, then a long, leisurely lunch before we get the ferry back.'

Aurora simply couldn't control the dawning of sheer delight in her eyes. 'I love Point Lookout,' she said helplessly.

He took her hand. 'Then why don't you get your costume, a hat and some sunscreen?'

'What about you?'

'My gear is in the car.'

'All right. But I'll need my hand back,' she responded with a mischievous glint in her eyes.

He looked down at her hand and thought how small it looked in his, then his dark gaze drifted all over her. And it occurred to him that it was true—he wasn't normally attracted to small girls, but this one could be an entirely different matter.

'Thank you for a wonderful day,' Aurora said as the Saab pulled up outside her town house much later that day. 'Would…would you like to come in?'

Luke shook his head, but slid his arm along the back of her seat. 'Thank *you* for a wonderful day, but I've got some work to do. And just to reassure you that I do keep my word…' He used his other hand to open the glove box and he pulled out two packets, which he put in her lap. 'Only two to go,' he murmured.

Aurora looked down at her diaries in her lap, and came tumbling down from the clouds. 'OK,' she heard herself say, 'I guess I'll hear from you when…whenever.'

'Aurora—'

'No. A deal is a deal, Luke. Goodnight.' She had her bag at her feet, which expedited a swift departure, but, for that matter, after one restless movement he didn't try to stop her, although he didn't drive off until she'd opened her door and switched on a light.

Then she did hear the Saab roar away and she walked dazedly into her lounge to curl up in her wing chair and rub her face miserably.

It had been a wonderful day. They'd done everything he'd suggested, but it hadn't only been the beauty of North Stradbroke Island and Point Lookout or the surf they'd swum in, the long lunch or the ferry rides across a placid and lovely Moreton Bay that had made it so magical. It had been Luke Kirwan.

The gorgeous but dangerous man on the prowl she'd seen the night of his house-warming had not been much in evidence, although she had found herself suddenly the object of palpable envy from her own sex throughout the day. But he'd also made her feel intensely alive and as if she was operating on all cylinders because he was mentally challenging to be with. They'd talked a lot during the day about all sorts of subjects.

Other things had appeared to be, mysteriously, more stimulating too. The wonderful seafood they'd eaten for lunch had acquired an almost sensuous quality to be eating it with him while they'd also enjoyed a bottle of wine. The thick grass beneath her bare feet as they'd strolled through the old Dunwich cemetery while they'd been waiting for the ferry home, the lovely old trees, the timelessness of the One Mile anchorage where the ferry came in—it had all sung to her very soul because he'd been there with her.

But, despite being surprisingly easy to handle, he was also physically challenging, she had to acknowledge. She'd discovered during the day that Luke Kirwan was breathtakingly beautifully put together. In fact, that was just what it had done—taken her breath away when they'd stripped to their costumes on the beach and the lean, clean, strong lines of his body had been revealed to her.

And when they'd come out of the water to stand side by side on the sand, sleek and dripping, she'd found she'd been able to feel and taste as if they were doing it, the final act of intimacy between a man and a woman. But beyond a lurking glint in his dark eyes as they'd skimmed her slim figure in a rose-pink bikini that had told her she was equally desirable, no more had come of it.

And now this, she thought bleakly, coming back to the present. She looked across the room to where she'd put her diaries down. A calculated reminder that this was a game to him? It had to be. What was more she, incredibly foolishly, had done all the things, bar one, she'd accused him of trying to achieve with this game. Even to feeling disappointed that he hadn't come in for a nightcap and kissed her goodnight.

Two more dates, Aurora, she thought unhappily, and you won't know if you're on your head or your heels and all over a blackmailer. There has to be a way out of this...

Perhaps he had never had any intention of reading her diaries, she wondered suddenly with a faint spark of hope. But it subsided almost immediately. Even if that were true, she was still under siege for whatever reason, but it didn't seem likely to be a long-term commitment.

If nothing else he was on the rebound—how many times had she had that pointed out to her, after all? And there was something about his own reticence on the subject that was... She considered for a moment. A little scary?

There was only one way to find out, she told herself. Was she game to throw down the gauntlet? No more dates until she got her remaining diaries back?

CHAPTER FIVE

THE next morning, out of the blue, Neil approached her with an exciting proposition—a talk-back show of her own.

'You mean I host it?' She stared at him wide-eyed.

'Yes—don't look so surprised.' He grinned. 'Once a week is what we have in mind with a guest in the studio who you will chat to first, then we'll open up the lines. We'll provide you with a research-assistant-cum-secretary. And the choice of guests will be something you and I will hammer out together; but we feel you're well-enough informed, you're well-enough travelled, certainly articulate enough, et cetera, to handle it and you're obviously of good character. But it will be a lot more work. How say you, Miss Templeton?'

'I say yes!' Aurora beamed back at him. 'This is *wonderful*—thank you, Neil!'

'My pleasure! Er—how's it going with Luke?'

Aurora stilled and felt a lot of her euphoria evaporate. 'Why?' she asked cautiously.

'I believe Leonie is mounting a reconciliation movement.'

'Oh.'

Neil raised an eyebrow. 'Are you still seeing him?'

Aurora rose. 'Not anymore, Neil. At least—not after tonight.'

'Aurora—'

'Neil—' she smiled down at him '—don't worry. Without so many people to keep me informed, I'd be working in the dark!' And she went to walk out jauntily but stopped in her tracks. 'What has good character got to do with it?' she asked with a frown.

'Well, the public wouldn't take kindly to a bank robber on their air space, and, once you open the lines to them, if you do have a skeleton in your closet someone could well embarrass you on air with it.' He eyed her humorously. 'So now's the time to come clean if there is anything deep and dark in your past, Aurora!'

'No, there's nothing...'

Nothing but an open police file on me and two of my diaries still in Luke Kirwan's possession, she thought for the tenth time in the space of an hour as she paced her lounge when she got home from work. So what to do?

Just go and explain things to him? If nothing else, it would prove to her once and for all what kind of a man he really was. But, say he was the devil in disguise, she mused, wouldn't she be handing him a real hold over her that could affect her career for ever?

She sat down and rubbed her temples distractedly. Most of her instincts told her that Luke Kirwan would drop this game if she put her case fairly and squarely. But, as was faithfully recorded in one of the diaries he still had, her one previous relationship with a man had proven beyond doubt that her instincts, on the subject of men, were not that reliable. At twenty-three she'd thought she'd fallen deeply in love but it had turned sour on her.

The love of her life had turned into a frighteningly possessive, jealous man and she'd had to fall back on her father to help to extricate her from the relationship...

Her father! She sat up suddenly. Even if she could just talk to him on his satellite phone! But she slumped back almost immediately—what would that achieve, other than worrying the life out of him wherever he was—which was somewhere in the middle of the Pacific Ocean?

Then her phone rang and it was Luke with a proposition. Barry and Julia were having a house party on the family sheep station, Beltrees, the coming weekend, and Julia had rung to ask if he would like to take Aurora.

'You're kidding!' Aurora said flatly.

'No,' he replied. 'And we'd fly so you'd still be able to work on Friday and Monday. I think you'd like Beltrees. And most people fall for my father although, I should warn you, he's a bit of a character.'

'He...would be there?' Aurora asked cautiously.

'Certainly.' He paused and when he went on she could hear the amusement in his voice. 'I think this would definitely qualify as a two-diary date, Aurora, and, well, it's entirely up to you what happens from then on.'

'I...see,' she said slowly.

There was a short silence, then, 'Are you all right, Aurora?'

She made a concentrated effort to perk up. 'I'm fine! OK. It sounds...fun.'

'Good. I'll get in touch later in the week. Bye.'

'Bye!' She put the phone down and stared at it with a most curious thought in her mind in the circumstances—what about Leonie's reconciliation attempt?

They flew to Beltrees in a light plane that belonged to the property.

During the preceding days, she'd worked hard on the approach she should take over this weekend and had decided that since she'd got three of her diaries back by being, mostly, herself, that was how she should continue. If she could, she'd thought several times, because things were much more serious now. It therefore came as a pleasant surprise to find that Beltrees itself was a help...

Situated between Charleville and Quilpie in south western Queensland, the station was in the heart of sheep country and, while it could be prone to drought, or flood, while it was often flat and not very interesting country, Aurora was in for a pleasant surprise. A good preceding season had turned it into a carpet of wild flowers.

'I can't believe it,' she said wonderingly of the splashes of lovely colour on the red soil as they floated down to land.

'You're lucky,' Luke said. 'It doesn't happen often like this.'

'Only every seven years or so,' the pilot contributed. 'OK, here we go.' He touched the plane down gently and they rolled to a stop at the end of a dirt strip. 'You're the last of the party to arrive,' he added.

'Who exactly is in the party?' Aurora enquired as they drove in an open four-wheel drive past a picturesque old wooden shearing shed and yards.

'Not sure.' Luke shrugged. 'All Julia said was that they were having a house party and would I like to bring you? But she comes from a big family.' In jeans, a khaki bush shirt and short boots with a broad-brimmed Akubra on the seat beside him, he fitted into the landscape well.

'Did you grow up here, Luke?' she asked.

'I did. And broke my father's heart when all I wanted to do was escape.' He looked around, then down at Aurora with a smile lurking at the back of his eyes. 'Sheep bore me to tears. On the other hand, it was a marvellous spot to observe the heavens.'

'So that's how it all started? With a passion for astronomy?'

'Mmm… But also phenomena such as artesian basins, water tables and rivers that run inland like Cooper Creek. So my time wasn't exactly wasted. Here we are.'

He pulled the vehicle up and Aurora blinked because Beltrees homestead was about as far from a typical Queensland homestead as one could get. Built of sandstone, it was long and low, had a steep red roof with a central gable, also sandstone, all the window frames were wood and it looked like trout lodge from the Scottish Highlands rather than a farmhouse in outback Queensland.

This impression was reinforced by the fact that the house, framed to the rear by trees, looked out over a lake, complete with swans, beyond a smooth green lawn.

'Luke!' she said in awed tones. 'Are you sure you're not

mad? This is incredible. Is there anything else you haven't told me?'

'Such as?'

'Well, it's not only incredible, it simply shouts—now I come to think of it,' she said on a descending scale, 'Neil did mention something about old money and family homes. I see what he means!' She turned to him urgently. 'I only brought one dress, all the rest are jeans and shorts.'

He laughed. 'You don't have to worry about clothes. When my mother was alive, she liked things to be, well, formal, but Julia is much more easygoing. By the way, my father is a little absent-minded—he often speaks his thoughts aloud, so don't be surprised. But he doesn't stand on ceremony and he hates people calling him Sir David.'

Aurora's mouth fell open. 'Sir David Kirwan? Knighted for his contribution to the wool industry? How come I never connected you to him?'

Before Luke had the chance to answer, Julia and Barry, with several dogs at their heels, came to meet them. And it was not until much later that night that Aurora was alone with Luke again, although she did find herself alone with Julia for a few minutes when Julia showed her to her room. Nor did Julia desert her outspokenness.

She said, 'You might be a little surprised about this, Aurora?'

'I am, Julia. Especially since I've been told Leonie wants him back.'

Julia sat down on the bed and grimaced. 'Don't hate me for this, but it wasn't my idea. Barry insisted I ask you. But then, for some strange reason, Barry was never a great fan of Leonie's and he has also insisted that I stay out of it. So, welcome to Beltrees, Aurora, and please don't feel you need to be wary of me.' She smiled what appeared to be a very genuine smile.

Aurora smiled back after overcoming a moment of complete surprise. She also thought—Good on you, Barry! At least one of you is prepared to judge me on my merits. It was only some time later that it occurred to her this was an inappropriate sentiment…

It wasn't a big house party by Beltrees standards, Aurora discovered.

Two other couples, one of which comprised Julia's sister and brother-in-law. The second couple were friends from the district and Aurora was the only stranger in their midst. But everyone welcomed her enthusiastically, almost overpoweringly so, in fact. Because she was not Leonie Murdoch, she surmised with an inward little grimace, but they were all trying to put it out of their minds?

She didn't get to meet Sir David until they were gathered in the lounge for pre-dinner drinks, and he was a different matter.

Fortunately, the one dress Aurora had brought was a little black number, sleeveless and round-necked, then A-line to just above her knees. It was quite plain but classy, and she tied her hair back with a tissuey gold scarf. The only problem was shoes, of which she had a nice black pair, patent with a narrow gold rim around the sole, but they were almost flat. Oh, well, she thought, there was nothing to be done about it, but she would have loved a bit of height.

And despite Luke's claims of Julia being much more easygoing than his mother, it was an elegant company that assembled in the lounge before dinner. In fact, it was an elegant house filled with marvellous antique furniture and paintings, and sherry was served from a crystal decanter.

Then a tall old man with a shock of white hair and shaggy eyebrows strode into the room, saying, 'OK, where is she? If she's ousted Leonie, she must be something else!'

'Dad,' Barry protested, 'I thought we agreed that subject was taboo—oh, hell!' he added helplessly.

'As a matter of fact, she is something else,' Luke said smoothly, into the awkward little pause that had developed.

'May I present Aurora Templeton?' He took Aurora's hand and drew her forward.

Aurora swallowed for some reason and looked up into a pair of dark eyes not unlike Luke's. 'How do you do?' she said politely. 'I've been told not to call you Sir David, but I don't know what else to call you.'

'Good Lord!' David Kirwan studied Aurora intently, from her tied-back streaky fair hair to her black patent shoes, then turned to Luke. 'Is this cradle-snatching or what?'

'She's twenty-five,' Luke murmured. 'As I recall, you were fifteen years older than Mum.'

'But...' Luke's father turned back to Aurora '...well, she couldn't be more different from Leonie if she tried!'

'So I've been told,' Aurora remarked, 'although, never having met the lady, I'm unable to form my own opinion. But she obviously has a formidable reputation—I wouldn't let my lack of inches fool you, however,' she added with a sparkle in her green eyes. 'I actually broke into your son's house once, knocked him out, and I haven't been able to get rid of him ever since.'

'Aurora,' Luke said gravely, 'that is playing with the truth a little.'

She turned her gaze to him. 'It's what you yourself accused me of, Luke,' she responded equally gravely.

'By gosh, a right sassy little one!' David Kirwan gazed down at Aurora. 'Do you know, I think I might see what he sees in you. And, come to think of it, Leonie's last tip on the stock market was a lousy one.'

Everyone started to laugh and David Kirwan took Aurora's hand and led her into dinner.

'You bowled my father right over,' Luke said when they were strolling, at his suggestion, beside the lake before going to bed.

'Oh, I think it would be fairer to say he's reserving judgement,' Aurora replied, and stopped to gaze at the reflection of the house lights on the smooth, dark surface of the water. And when she shivered because the night was cool, he took his jacket off and put it around her.

'Maybe, but he's enjoying himself along the way.'

'He's rather a sweetie.' They came to a bench and she sank down on it. 'What a marvellous night. It's a little hard to associate this—' she waved a hand '—with the dust and rigours of an outback sheep station.'

'Plenty of blood, sweat and tears went into the creation of Beltrees. But my father had the foresight to diversify into other things rather than ride completely on a sheep's back.'

'Did you break his heart, Luke?' She looked up at him as he stood before her on the lake's edge.

'Not really. Barry is more than happy to take my place and I still keep an eye on the business side of things.'

'I would have thought you were a son to be proud of.'

He shrugged. 'I suspect he has grandchildren on his mind these days. Barry and Julia don't seem to be in any hurry to provide them and I'm definitely…dragging my heels.'

She thought for a moment, about how Luke had been during the evening, and wondered about the disenchantment she'd sensed in him. Not that it was anything to concern her, she told herself. She had one clear goal to concentrate on, and why, for example, he might have decided to present her to his father should not be allowed to deflect her from that goal. All the same…

She patted the bench beside her. 'Sit down for a moment,' she invited, 'and tell me which star is what.'

He grinned and sat down. 'There's the Southern Cross—'

'I know *that*—are you feeling dangerous again, Luke?'

He was silent for a long moment, then, 'How did you know?'

'I could tell you were dangerous from the first moment I met you—remember? Although that was in a different context, of course, but some of the signs are the same—a bored sort of arrogant aura. Is it…was it because your father brought up Leonie?'

He slid his arm along the back of the bench, around her shoulders. 'We do antagonize each other sometimes, Dad and I. He's not quite as absent-minded as he would like everyone to think—the Leonie reference was no doubt a well-thought-out ploy to point out the error of my ways to me.'

'Why did you bring me along, then?' Aurora queried. 'You must have had some idea that it would happen.'

'Because it seemed like a good idea to get it over and done with.'

Aurora grimaced and unthinkingly laid her cheek on his shoulder. Then she realised what she was doing and went to sit up, but he stilled her.

'Relax,' he said. 'No one can see us.'

'It wasn't that…' She paused. 'Perhaps I *feel* like the error of your ways now.'

He laughed softly. 'On the other hand, you couldn't be more aptly named for an astrophysicist, which is my speciality. I guess you know what Aurora means?' He looked down at her.

'The dawn—I was born just as the sun rose!'

'A little bundle of joy. But in meteorological terms an aurora is a luminous, sometimes richly coloured display of arcs, bands and streamers in the sky and there are two famous ones: aurora borealis and aurora australis. That's how I'm coming to think of you—as my aurora australis.'

She caught her breath for a moment and looked up at the night sky with a feeling of wonder in her heart but caution prevailed. 'As well as the error of your ways?' she suggested gravely.

'Actually, that's the last thing you feel like at the moment.' He stroked her cheek with his fingertips.

She knew she should resist, but when he drew her closer she found she simply couldn't.

'How does that feel?' he asked.

She shrugged. 'You're rather nice to lean against. You make me feel safe—I mean,' she sought to qualify it immediately, 'say there were wild animals roaming about out there, I'd be much happier to have you around than to be here alone.'

She felt the jolt of laughter that ran through him, then he was quiet for a time. 'Do you often feel unsafe and lonely, Aurora?' he asked at last.

She hesitated.

'One thing that struck me when I skimmed through your diaries, and has been reinforced since I got to know you, is that you've had some long, lonely periods in your life with no mother and your father gone frequently,' he said.

'I…perhaps,' she conceded, 'although I don't usually give it much thought. But it's a bit worse at the moment because my father is away sailing the high seas again, but he's alone this time and he's the only family I've got. Both he and my mother were only children and all my grandparents are gone. I don't know why this has struck me now,' she confessed and tilted her face to his. 'What made you bring it up?'

'It struck me this evening,' he said meditatively, 'that I'd rather have thrown you into the lion's den and, for a slip of a girl for whom, often, her diaries were her lifeline, you were extraordinarily brave—I don't why, but it did. The other thing that occurred to me was—that I would be only too happy to kiss you and make you feel safe.' He bent his head and sought her lips.

Several minutes later, as they drew apart, she was feeling quite different. Trembling with desire and conscious of an electric, physical tension between them as he ran his hands up and down her arms beneath his jacket and handled her in a way she was becoming achingly familiar with. A way that made her pulse-rate soar and filled her with a heady delight because he was strong and powerful, but he made her feel silken, beautiful and desirable.

'This is getting harder and harder to handle,' she breathed.

He cupped her shoulders, then withdrew his hands, closed his jacket up to her chin and took her loosely in his arms. 'But nice?' He rubbed his chin on the top of her head.

'Wonderful. I don't feel so much like the error of your ways any more. Still—'

'You're quite safe from me here at Beltrees,' he broke in quizzically.

'I know, but that's only two nights.'

'Perhaps we could come to a new arrangement after Beltrees.' He tilted her chin and kissed the tip of her nose.

'You know,' she said slowly, 'I'm trying to picture you as a little boy, staring up at the stars.'

'I'll show you my first telescope tomorrow. I made it myself.'

She looked at him wonderingly.

'In the meantime, however, if I'm to stick to my good intentions, perhaps we should go in?' he suggested.

They did, to their separate bedrooms, without speaking except to say goodnight. And it was as if they had an unseen, unspoken link between them, a mental association that was calm and close despite the separate rooms.

But it was a long time before Aurora got to sleep as she contemplated how foolish she'd been to kid herself she only had one goal—getting back her diaries...

The next day, a Saturday, was active.

A tour of the property on horseback, a barbecue for lunch, then tennis. Luke did also show her his first telescope during the afternoon, although it took quite a search through a box-room to find it.

'There.' He dusted it off. 'Pretty primitive! I don't know if it still works—the prisms may have gone haywire.'

'How did you have the knowledge to build it?' she asked, fascinated.

'I got the instructions out of a science magazine. I got a

lot of ideas from science magazines, some that caused me to get my hide tanned. Like the homemade rocket that set fire to the wool-shed roof.'

Aurora burst out laughing.

'Not funny,' he remarked. 'Oh, here's something that should interest you, a crystal radio set. I could actually tune into the flying doctor's frequency—hell, it's broken.'

'Luke, you should keep these properly,' she remonstrated. 'Your kids could be fascinated one day.'

He grimaced. 'It's junk, really. I don't think I've looked at them since I was about…fifteen.'

She closed her hand over his. 'Keep them. You never know. If they were my kids…' She stopped abruptly.

He looked down at her and she felt a tingling sensation down her spine and a rush of colour come to her cheeks. 'I wonder what kind of kids we would have?' he said idly. 'Sassy little girls not above breaking into other people's homes?'

'Or boys that set fire to the wool shed?' she countered, although she was still feeling flustered.

'Perhaps we'd filter out the worst of each other,' he suggested.

'I'm not admitting to any…criminal side that needs filtering out,' she said primly.

'Unless it suits you, Aurora. My father took me aside this morning and asked me if you really broke into my house.'

She looked rueful. 'What did you say?'

'That he should ask you.'

'Thanks! Uh…who knows?'

'What our children would be like? You're right.' He put his hands around her waist and lifted her up to sit her on the edge of a table, then proceeded to study her face enigmatically.

'I know what you're thinking,' she said after a moment. 'I was the one who made sweeping statements fairly recently about not being ready to surrender to marriage, maternity and domesticity—and now I'm talking kids, although it was in the most general way.'

He fiddled with the buttons of her pink blouse, then adjusted some tendrils of hair behind her ears. 'Nope! I wasn't thinking about that at all.'

'Oh. What, then?'

'The lovely sheen of your skin...' he trailed his fingers down her cheek '...the gloss of your lips; the way you hit a tennis ball, as if you'd like to fire it right through your opponent, and how you stick the tip of your tongue out at the same time. Those kind of things.'

'Luke—' she laughed '—I don't!'

'Yes, you do—you certainly are a pocket dynamo, Miss Templeton.'

'I suppose I am competitive,' she conceded.

'But a lot less aggressive on the subject of myself,' he remarked casually, although with an oddly acute little gleam in his eye.

She thought for a bit—with a feeling of being on dangerous ground. 'Perhaps, like your father, I'm reserving judgement.'

'Why?'

'You are still holding two of my diaries,' she pointed out.

'Ah, so this is a "good behaviour" version of Aurora Templeton until you get them back?' he suggested quizzically.

'Wouldn't you...have some plan of action if you were in my shoes?' she countered with some irony.

'Possibly.' He looked wry. 'Was kissing me last night part of your good-behaviour bond?'

She merely gazed at him.

'How about this, then? If there were only you and I at Beltrees, we could go for a swim in the lake without bothering about costumes, we could then make love on the grass, rest and recuperate a bit and have a candlelight supper for two whenever the mood took us.'

Aurora narrowed her eyes. 'I thought I was supposed to be safe from you at Beltrees?'

'We aren't alone,' he pointed out.

'Just as well, Professor,' she said sternly. 'I can see I would be in for a...decadent time otherwise.'

'I wouldn't call that decadent,' he drawled. 'I think it would be rather—delicious.' He kissed her lightly.

She slipped her hands around his neck. 'You're still in that dangerous mood, Mr Kirwan.'

'Could have a lot to do with you, Miss Templeton. Ah—' he paused as a gong sounded '—you're saved by the tea bell.'

Aurora groaned.

'That's highly complimentary,' he remarked, his eyes bright with devilry.

'I was only groaning because the thought of more food after that barbecue is enough to sink me!' she informed him.

'I'm demolished,' he murmured.

She kissed him back. 'No, you're not. In fact, you're still playing games with me, Luke. I haven't quite figured out what they are, but I will!' She removed his hands from her waist and slipped off the table. 'See you at tea,' she said pertly, and left him watching her with a rather wry expression.

But once she was out of sight, she paused to ask herself what kind of games *she* thought she was playing. And groaned inwardly this time.

The rest of their stay at Beltrees passed without incident— until a couple of hours before they were due to leave and Sir David fell off his horse and broke his arm, as well as concussing himself. With the result that he and Luke were flown to the Charleville hospital, and Aurora continued on alone to Brisbane.

She'd assured Luke that she quite understood and he was not to worry about her. He'd kissed her briefly and openly, and told her he'd be in touch as soon as he got back to Brisbane, himself.

She did wonder if he'd instruct Miss Hillier to return her diaries to her, but, when a few days went by and nothing happened, consoled herself with the thought that Luke probably had his safe keys on him. But when a few more days went by with no word from him, she began to feel tense and annoyed and, quite irrationally, not only on the subject of her diaries.

This was a man, after all, who made a habit of either kissing her or thinking about it, then leaving her dangling. Well, it was time she took a stand, she decided. So she rang Miss Hillier, discovered he was due home that day, and informed his secretary that she required an audience with him that evening, come hell or high water.

Miss Hillier demurred, and even protested that she had no control over his movements, but subsided when Aurora threatened to move into her old home.

She chose a severely tailored dark green linen suit for the appointment and wore black accessories. She put her hair up in a no-nonsense pleat and put on the minimum of make-up, then added a bit of blusher because she not only looked but felt a bit pale. Finally, there was nothing left to do but drive up the hill to her old home.

Miss Hillier let her in with an expression of concern on her face. 'He's not in a very good mood,' she said in little more than a whisper.

'Neither am I,' Aurora whispered back. 'All right, lead me into the lion's den.'

'He's just come in and he's on the phone. Take a seat in the lounge and I'll bring you a cup of—'

'Could you make that a brandy and soda?' Aurora requested. 'My moral fibre needs a bit of a boost.'

Surprisingly, Miss Hillier chuckled. 'I might even have one myself.'

*   *   *

Ten minutes later, when Aurora had half finished her brandy and soda, Luke strode into the lounge.

'Aurora,' he said abruptly, 'sorry to keep you waiting. And I'm sorry I haven't been in touch but complications set in—my father developed pneumonia.'

'Oh.' She bit her lip. 'I'm sorry. How—?'

'He's going to be all right, but it was touch and go for a while,' he interrupted, and his gaze fell on the glass beside her, then came back to rest on her face with a tinge of satire in those dark eyes. Nor was his manner of dress any consolation to Aurora. In a charcoal pinstripe suit with a pale grey shirt and dark tie, he was an impressive but distant figure.

He also said, with his gaze on the glass again, 'It would appear you've come on a mission, Aurora. Let me guess—your diaries?'

Aurora took a breath and wondered a little wildly how to proceed. In the light of his father's health he could conceivably be forgiven for forgetting her diaries, and normally she would have forgiven him, but that wasn't all there was between them—or was it? Why else would he not have contacted her? Why else would he be this formal, distant stranger to her now? Why should she be made to feel the last thing he needed on his mind was her and her diaries?

She swallowed, then forced herself to relax. 'I am very sorry to hear about your father, but I'd rather you didn't tower over me like this, Luke.'

He sat down opposite. 'Better?' This time there was a tinge of insolence in his expression.

She eyed him. 'I believe you're not in a very good mood?'

He smiled unamusedly. 'I believe you and Miss Hillier must be in cahoots again.' He looked at his watch. 'Unfortunately I have another appointment shortly, so could we get down to brass tacks?'

Aurora took a very deep breath this time. 'All right. This has gone on long enough. I want my diaries back *now*. I'm about to enter a new era of my life and I need to get this situation sorted out so—'

'All right.'

'So—what did you say?' Her eyes were huge suddenly.

'I'll get them.' He called Miss Hillier, handed over a set of keys to her and requested that she get the two remaining diaries out of his safe.

While they waited, with Aurora feeling slightly shell-shocked, he recommended that she finish her drink. She did so in one large gulp and, when Miss Hillier returned, accepted her diaries dazedly. Miss Hillier hesitated, glanced at her boss, then retreated, taking Aurora's glass with her.

'So—what's this new "era" of your life all about? It seems to have come up pretty suddenly,' he said.

Confusion made Aurora blink several times, then tell him. Once she had, she said hollowly, though, 'I wasn't going to go into the details.'

'Why not? It sounds like quite a coup for you.'

'All the more reason not to want—I mean, now my public profile—'

'I see,' he interrupted. 'You didn't want your diaries floating around out of your control in case I was tempted to—somehow—damage your public profile with them?'

She hesitated, then nodded.

He stood up and went to the terrace doors, where he stood for a while examining the view with his hands shoved into his pockets, then turned back to her. 'Is that the only reason?'

'Of course not,' she answered quietly, and willed herself to keep hold of her composure. 'I hate not knowing where I stand, I hate the thought of anyone reading them—and I don't much like the thought that you could be that kind of man.'

He grimaced. 'I never had the slightest intention of reading them.'

A little well of hope rose in Aurora's heart. She said,

however, 'I wasn't to know that and, even so, it was still a game you were playing with me.'

'And you're not into playing games with men?' he drawled.

Aurora narrowed her eyes. 'Certainly not men on the rebound—or on the prowl.'

He raised his eyebrows thoughtfully. 'Is that how it felt lately?'

'No,' she conceded after a moment, and with a tinge of pink in her cheeks. 'But then the "you" of lately is light years away from the "you" of now.'

He studied her smart suit and elegant shoes. 'I could say the same of you, Aurora.'

'Have you got back with Leonie—is that what all this is about?'

'Jealous, Aurora?' he queried softly.

She stood up and clenched her fists.

'Before you demolish me or try physically to put me in my place,' he said with patent, hateful amusement, 'if you'd never known about Leonie, what kind of a judgement would you have placed on us?'

She paused. 'How can I? I did know, I still know, so how can I make an unbiased judgement?'

'Surely you must have had some original thoughts into which Leonie didn't intrude? When you were kissing me, for example?' The insolence was right out in the open now.

She clenched her teeth this time. 'You're in an impossible mood! I'll remove my unwanted presence so you can get to your next appointment.'

'Your presence is not unwanted, Aurora. I'd like nothing better than to remove your "power dressing"—' his gaze roamed up and down her smart but severe suit '—incidentally I preferred your señorita outfit—and make love to you here and now.'

She gasped. 'How can you say that?'

'Easily, because it's true. Making love to you has become

something I think about rather a lot lately.' He smiled slightly. 'Why do you think I didn't come in after we'd been to Point Lookout? Why do you think I took you to Beltrees, amongst so many people, not the least my father?'

She found herself bereft of speech.

'That's why, Aurora,' he drawled with lethal satire.

'You know…you know what?' she said shakily. 'You're the kind of man who wants to have his cake and eat it—'

'More sayings, Aurora?' he mocked. 'You really are a gold mine of them.'

'Oh!' She picked up her bag and diaries. 'That's it. Don't you dare darken my door again, Luke Kirwan, and rest assured I shall take great pleasure in never having to lay eyes on you again!' She all but ran from the room and he didn't move a muscle to stop her.

Three days later as she read her morning news bulletin her mind was still almost as churned up as it had been when she'd run away from Luke. In fact, she was reading automatically until she came to an item that made her pause, stumble, then apologize and continue.

And when the news was finished, Neil, instead of giving her his usual thumbs up, asked her if she was OK because she looked a bit pale and sickly. She told him she was feeling that way, but didn't tell him why, and gratefully accepted his offer of the rest of the day off.

When she got home, she leant back against the front door and marvelled at her stupidity. She had completely forgotten, until she'd come to read an item about a home invasion, that the police still had an open file on her. And now that she'd seen the other side of Luke Kirwan, a side she'd hated, how could she be sure it wouldn't turn out to be the skeleton in her closet Neil had mentioned?

She spent the rest of the day arguing it out with herself but, in the end, there seemed to be only one thing to do.

CHAPTER SIX

THIS time she made no appointment with Miss Hillier.

She drove up the hill, rang the bell, then knocked on the front door. There was no response but there were lights on in the house so she walked round and let herself in through the sliding doors that opened onto the terrace. And she had no intimation that she was about to encounter the scholarly side of Luke Kirwan, but that was what happened.

He'd mentioned to her that he'd had the billiard room converted to a study, and that was where she found him, at his desk, surrounded by a sea of papers with his hair rumpled and blue shadows on his jaw.

He looked up as she appeared in the doorway, and blinked.

'I rang the bell and I knocked,' she said. 'I'm sorry if you were deliberately ignoring them in case it was me, but—'

'I...no,' he broke in. 'I didn't hear them.'

She frowned at him.

'No, I haven't suddenly gone deaf, I just switch off and ignore things like that when I'm working. Sorry.'

'Oh.'

'But I must admit this is a surprise,' he said after a moment and stood up to come round the desk.

It came as something of a shock to Aurora—her inward reaction to the lean, untidy length of him in faded jeans and an old sweatshirt. Nothing detracted from the fact that the way he was put together was sleek, powerful and simply awesome, she thought with a little pulse of panic. Nor did it help her to be subjected to a brief scrutiny up and down her figure and have an eyebrow slightly raised at her conservative attire—khaki cargo pants and a loose check shirt with long sleeves.

'I came because I forgot something,' she said stiffly.

His mouth curved into a wicked grin. 'Not more diaries, Aurora?'

'No. The police file. It's really important to me, because of my new programme that it…that you retract it, or something.' She twisted her hands together.

'Oh, that.' He gestured casually. 'I had it expunged weeks ago. Before our first "date", as a matter of fact.'

Her eyes widened and her mouth dropped open. 'How?'

'I told the police that it was a misunderstanding of a…domestic nature.'

'What?'

He smiled faintly at her incredulous expression. 'A dispute between myself and a…lady friend who had come back to claim some of her property but, on finding the front door open, she decided to dispense with making her presence known to me and just nip in and retrieve her things.'

'You…they *bought* that? In the middle of the night, with a torch, et cetera, et cetera?'

'Lovers who have fallen out are renowned for doing strange things,' he said and looked at her meaningfully.

'So—so—' Aurora had difficulty getting her words out '—I'm now down on the record as being your estranged lover? That's…diabolical!'

'Would you prefer to be down on the record as a burglar?'

'Of course not! No…but…' She trailed off and stared at him, breathing heavily.

'It so happens,' he said after a moment, 'your actual name is not down on any record. They quite understood that my natural gallantry, despite having fallen out with you, precluded me wanting to name you.'

She opened her mouth, shut it, then said feebly, 'Well, thanks. I didn't think you had much natural gallantry, to be honest, but…' She hesitated.

He said nothing, just observed her idly although somehow comprehensively until the heat began to rush beneath her skin again.

'All right!' She closed her eyes. 'That was gallant! But...' She stopped frustratedly.

'Uh—could I offer you a drink?' he suggested and, without waiting for a reply, invited her to sit down while he got it.

She looked around with a frown of concentration while she waited, and a deep feeling of uncertainty because she'd obviously misjudged him, but that didn't explain away their last encounter...

He'd had the billiard room completely redecorated. Two walls were lined floor to ceiling with bookshelves and stuffed with books, and a third had a built-in desk and shelves that housed an impressive display of computer-ware. The main desk was free-standing and massive and situated so he could see the view from the window but, by simply swivelling his chair round, he was able to work on his computer.

She was sitting on a leather couch with a coffee-table in front of it, and in front of the window stood a powerful telescope. All the woodwork was beautifully done, the colour scheme of carpet, curtains and the free wall space was a restful combination of mossy green and copper and the main desk was a beauty, mahogany with many drawers and curved brass handles.

But the aura of the room was much more than tasteful, and not particularly restful. It was very obviously the home of a probing intellect, of a man who had admitted to her that running sheep stations bored him rigid and shown her his first telescope that he'd built when he was ten.

Then he came back with two drinks and sat down beside her.

Aurora took a sip of brandy and soda and said, 'I'm sorry if I—'

'Did you honestly think I'd use that against you, Aurora?'

She closed her mouth, and sighed. 'I didn't know what to think. But, to be honest, after the last time I came here I wasn't, well, I didn't know what to think,' she repeated helplessly.

'Ah. It would be handy if I could expunge that from the record,' he murmured and looked down at her, 'but I was under a bit of pressure, unfortunately.'

'Because of your father? Well, I can see that now, I guess.'

He smiled dryly. 'You're very generous, Aurora. And it was because of my father, but not quite in the way you might imagine. Of course, I was really concerned for his health but…a sudden brush with mortality brought out a strange reaction in him. He told me it was his dearest wish to see me married and settled down before he departed this life.'

Aurora did a doubletake.

'Quite,' he agreed ruefully, then changed the subject. 'Have you eaten yet?'

'Uh…no.' She shook her head.

'Neither have I. How about scrambled eggs on toast?'

'You…could do that? What about all this work you were so deeply engrossed in?' She looked across at the desk.

He grimaced. 'I wasn't getting anywhere with it.' But his gaze returned to his desk as well with something a touch regretful in it.

'Tell you what,' Aurora said, 'why don't I make the scrambled eggs while you capture any last thoughts you may have on whatever it is that's so elusive?'

He turned back to her, took her chin in his fingers, and kissed her lingeringly. 'You are a peach,' he said softly.

But when Aurora had made her escape to the kitchen, she stood for a long moment with her hands on her still-flushed cheeks and a sense of bemusement in her heart because she'd fallen right back under Luke Kirwan's spell without even trying…

*   *   *

'I'm working on a speech,' he told her after they'd eaten from trays on their knees in the den, 'that I've been asked to present as the opening address to an international conference on astrophysics to be held on the Gold Coast in two weeks. I'm trying to…blend the old with the new, I guess. Draw a line from Ptolemy, Copernicus, Galileo, Halley, Newton, et cetera to the modern day.'

'Ah, I know a bit about that,' Aurora said. 'I've just finished a lovely book, *Galileo's Daughter*. I also read another of Dava Sobell's books, *Longitude*, and found it fascinating, as a sailor's daughter. So I'm actually a mine of information, contrary to what you might have suspected, Professor.'

He looked amused, then thoughtful. 'Galileo's daughter…'

'Does that give you inspiration?' she asked.

'Well, it's obviously been done so—and not that I'm suggesting she was humorous—but my speech, because it's the opening address rather than a paper, needs a bit of humour—'

'I'm not sure about Ptolemy. Copernicus was a monk but maybe Isaac Newton or Edmund Halley had a wife that you could draw some humour from?' Aurora broke in to suggest. 'Mind you, it was quite customary in Galileo's days, at least, for scholars not to marry. That's why his daughters ended up in a nunnery—they were illegitimate and didn't have any prospects because of it. You don't—' She broke off and glinted a wicked little look at him. '*You* don't subscribe to that view, do you, Luke?'

'Not at all,' he denied and shrugged. 'I've never thought about it that way.'

'So why did you and Leonie call it quits?' Aurora heard herself ask.

He blinked at her.

Aurora wrinkled her nose. 'Sorry. That just slipped out. Well, it *is* topical, I guess. And I'm reliably informed she's a ten, if not to say an eleven or twelve, Leonie Murdoch.'

'Who by? Don't tell me—Neil and Mandy Pearson.'

Aurora agreed wryly. 'To compound matters, Neil couldn't have been more surprised to hear you and I were walking out together than if I'd told him the…the Aga Khan had taken an interest in me.'

'I think the present one *would* be a little old for you, Aurora.'

She ignored the little glint of irony in his eyes and gestured. 'You know what I mean. He seemed to think we were in different leagues. He also, now I come to think of it, expressed the opinion of you that—no.' Aurora stopped.

'Please don't spare my feelings,' Luke said politely.

'It's not your feelings I'm worried about,' she retorted. 'I just don't feel right about quoting what Neil said in confidence, I guess.'

'Then I'll ask him—you have spilt most of the beans anyway.'

'Luke!' Aurora stood up and put her tray on the coffee-table. 'Don't you dare!'

'There is, actually, no way you could stop me, Aurora,' he murmured. He stood up. 'In fact I might give him a ring right now.'

She looked around a little wildly. 'There's no phone in this room!' And she walked over to the doorway and stood in it with her arms akimbo.

'I know you knocked me out once, but are you seriously suggesting you're capable of barring me into this room?' he queried.

'You knocked yourself out!'

'Aurora—' he came to stand in front of her '—it so happens I was indisposed that night, not to mention wondering whether I was hallucinating. I'm perfectly fit and in my right mind at the moment.'

She looked up at him. 'Is that a threat, Luke?'

'Of a sort,' he said gravely. 'Apart from having something to prove dating back to our first encounter, I can't think of anything I'd rather be doing—than this.' He picked her up and carried her over to a leather settee.

She wriggled in his arms, more from surprise than anything else, but immediately knew she had as much chance of escaping him as getting out of a steel trap. 'I don't propose,' she told him as he sat down with her in his lap, 'to engage in any undignified, not to mention wasted struggles, Luke Kirwan. And I have to point out that you more than avenged yourself for that first night on the very next occasion we met. I also don't intend to succumb to—more blackmail.'

'No? What do you think I have in mind?'

She pretended to consider. 'Kissing me into some kind of submission?'

He grinned at her. 'What a lovely prospect!'

'But you wouldn't—would you, Luke?'

'I certainly had in mind kissing you. If you regard it as a fate worse than death—' his dark eyes glinted '—all you have to do is tell me what Neil said.'

'Try me,' she suggested, a little glint in her own eyes.

'That is throwing down the gauntlet, Aurora.'

She merely composed her features, closed her eyes and clasped her hands at her waist. But he didn't attempt to kiss her immediately. He played with the top button of her shirt, then slid his fingers beneath it and cupped her shoulder.

She resisted the tremors threatening to run through her with an almost Herculean effort of will. She told herself she must be mad—how had she allowed herself to fall into this kind of game with him? But when he slipped her bra strap aside and stroked her breast, she had to bite her lip to give her will power a bit of a boost. And when her nipples peaked, when she moved convulsively at the aching delight he was wreaking on her body, she had to admit she was unequal to the gauntlet she'd thrown down.

Her lashes flew up and she said raggedly, 'He thought, because you've always had women chasing after you, that the concept of monogamy might be a little foreign to you. Luke—' she sat up '—if you ever tell him I told you or let it interfere with your friendship, I'll never forgive you! He was only theorizing because—' she gestured helplessly '—no one could understand why you and Leonie had parted, I guess. You've never made me feel quite like that before, not even at Beltrees,' she added.

'I'm glad it rated a mention.'

Some colour ran beneath her skin as he adjusted her shirt and kissed her chastely. Then she lay back against his arm, which was propped along the armrest of the settee, and studied him. 'You may not be the devil in disguise I took you for, over my diaries and the police file, but there's still so much I don't know or understand.'

'Such as, not being at all sure you want to go down this road with a man to whom the concept of monogamy may be foreign?' he suggested.

She stared into his dark eyes, her own suddenly wide. 'Is it?'

'Of course not.' He lifted his head and looked across the room.

'So—what did go wrong with Leonie?' she asked.

It was a long moment before he brought his gaze back to her. 'Does this indicate a renewed interest in getting to know me, Aurora?'

She chewed her lip for a moment, then looked at him sideways to a quizzical little glint in his eyes. 'After what has just occurred, it may be a little difficult for you to grasp that I still have reservations about that, Luke,' she replied formally, 'but I do.'

'I quite understand,' he said gravely.

She clicked her teeth shut, then said through them, 'No, you don't!

In fact, that is a prime example of a male chauvinist at his worst—what you just said.'

His lips twitched, but before he could respond she went

on intensely, 'Everyone, and I do mean *everyone*, who knows us has exhibited either intense surprise that I should be putting myself in Leonie's shoes, or intense concern for her. What the hell am I to think?' she asked. 'Apart from the obvious—that we must be as different as chalk from cheese.'

'You are,' he murmured, trailing the tips of his fingers down her cheek.

'How so?' she asked, a little stunned.

He moved restlessly and Aurora sat up and slipped off his lap so she was sitting beside him.

And she said quietly, when he didn't answer, 'Maybe not such a threat to your independence as Leonie was?'

'You're actually a considerable threat to my peace of mind, Aurora,' he replied with a trace of humour. 'But I wasn't intending to do anything about it until—' his lips quirked '—you walked into my trap over the matter of Neil.'

She said crossly, 'I should have known better.' Then a lightening smile lit her eyes, but she sobered suddenly. 'It doesn't get me any further forward, though.'

Luke stood up and walked over to his desk, where he pushed some papers around for a moment, then he turned to her. 'I don't know what went wrong,' he said. 'I had the greatest admiration for Leonie, I thought I was in love with her, I went along with her plans for the future in so much as—in the fullness of time we would get married. I even...' he paused and looked around '...bought this house with an eye to that kind of future. Then I got cold feet. For some reason it was like looking down the barrel of a gun.'

Aurora blinked.

He shrugged. 'Perhaps I should rephrase: there was something niggling away at me that I could only identify as a disinclination to change our—*modus operandi*.'

'So you would have been happy to go on as before but

not marry her?' Aurora asked. 'That's…' She couldn't continue.

He smiled briefly. 'Diabolical? She thought so too and I can't blame her. But that's what happened, Aurora. Perhaps you'd like to make a judgement? Although, believe me, it has nothing to do with requiring more than one wife.'

'Just a disinclination to be tied down by any one woman for the rest of your life,' Aurora said more to herself than him, then she looked at him penetratingly. 'You could be more like Galileo and the scholars of his time than you know. Wedded to your science, kind of thing, so that any woman could only take second place.'

'Only time will tell, I imagine,' he replied, a touch dryly.

'You object to me doing this? You did invite me to make a judgement, Luke. And you did, or do, seem to have a rather personal interest in me despite coming close to getting your fingers burnt with Leonie Murdoch—darn it,' she said. 'Does she know about me?'

'If Mandy Pearson or Julia have anything to do with it, I'm quite sure Leonie does—' his tone was even dryer than earlier '—but I haven't tried to hide you—why would I?'

'There's a difference between being open and above board—and flaunting a new girlfriend,' Aurora said distractedly. 'I keep getting back to how soon—'

'Aurora, the reason it happened so soon is because you precipitated it.'

'I *didn't*, I—'

But he broke in again, 'You certainly came to my notice in a rather dramatic way. You certainly made sure it wouldn't be a forgettable encounter—the first one or the second one.'

She gasped. 'I didn't do any of that deliberately! I was desperately trying to avoid you, Luke Kirwan!'

'I know, I know. What I'm trying to say is—things just happened that way. Whereas you seem to feel it was all part of some devious plot on my part—to what? That's where you lose me.'

'Perhaps you should have waited a while,' she said helplessly at last. 'And now this. Your father's worried about you, Leonie wants a reconciliation—is that true, by the way?'

He looked at her but didn't answer for a long moment. 'Leonie seems to think we've thrown three good years away for no real reason,' he said at last. 'I'm not so sure. Aurora, could we talk about you for a change?'

'Why? I mean…what do you want to know?' She held his dark gaze steadily although she was reeling inwardly from his honesty.

He leant against the edge of the desk, crossed his long legs and folded his arms. 'How experienced are you, Aurora?'

She sat down on the settee rather abruptly and clasped her hands together. Then she said slowly, 'I see what you mean—how my expectations and previous experience of men might colour my dealings with you? I'm much less complicated than you are, Luke.' She smiled briefly. 'Several teenage infatuations, then a serious crush, but he was a married man so—he never even knew about it. That's one reason I was so determined to get my diaries back unread—as you probably know,' she said ruefully.

He put his head to one side. 'I must have missed that bit. I didn't read them in detail, I told you.'

'Enough to know…' She stopped and looked away.

'To sense they were a lifeline—yes. Go on,' he said gently after a moment.

'At twenty-three, I took the plunge. In retrospect, I think I was beginning to feel like the last spinster on the planet because it all seemed to blow up out of the blue. At the time I thought This Was It, in capitals, but six months later—well—' she raised her eyebrows '—maybe I'm not so unlike you after all. I began to feel stifled, he became possessive and jealous—over nothing—and I found myself in the uncomfortable position of asking myself what I had ever seen in him. Strange,' she mused.

He was watching her narrowly. 'Perhaps even frightening?'

'Yes, even frightening. I had to hide behind my father, in fact, to extricate myself.'

He smiled faintly. 'That would have gone against the grain.'

She looked wry. 'I do like to fight my own battles, but I was extremely grateful to have Dad do it for me.'

'And do you think any residue of it has coloured your dealings with men since?'

'Yes, it has,' she said honestly, then glinted him a wicked little look. 'As you know, I have strong feelings about being smitten on first encounters and I'm always on the lookout against…'

'Being led down the garden path,' he finished for her. 'Is that all?'

She said serenely, 'It hasn't turned me off men, as you might have noticed, but it would be fair to say I'm older and quite a bit wiser because of it. There hasn't been anyone serious since then.'

He straightened. 'So, how do *you* see us?'

'Ah. I really don't know. Isn't that why this all came up?'

'How would it be,' he suggested slowly, 'if we carried on as before until some clarification comes to us?'

Aurora took her time in answering as a little voice inside her said, Don't do this, Aurora. He may not be the devil in disguise but there's no guarantee you wouldn't get hurt… When was there any guarantee of that, though? she asked herself and looked around—a mistake, as it turned out. Because she encountered the other side of Luke Kirwan that was starting to fascinate her: his scholarly side.

'You mean, more as friends?' she asked uncertainly. 'If

that's what you mean, we'd have to draw the line at what went on in here earlier,' she added with more spirit.

'As in—I'm not allowed to lay a finger on you?' he queried with a wicked little glint.

'Mae West,' she said tartly, 'was of this opinion—Give a man a free hand and he'll try to put it all over you.'

He came over and sat down beside her laughing quietly. But after a moment, he said, 'We could stop here and now, Aurora, if you really wanted to.'

'Is that...how little it means to you?' she asked with a quiver in her voice that she couldn't hide.

He put an arm around her. 'No. It means a lot to me. You may not realize this but I feel a lot more relaxed, a lot less—' his lips twisted '—*dangerous* since getting to know you.'

She leant back against him. 'Really?'

'Really. But—'

'No, don't go on,' she said. 'I think I understand and I feel quite complimented—I probably shouldn't,' she mused. 'I probably should even feel like a pair of carpet slippers—'

'There is not the slightest comparison,' he drawled. 'You are...like a breath of fresh air in my life.'

'Thanks. I guess I have to say that in between making my life a misery, there have been one or two bright spots—but perhaps we should leave it there, for the time being, Professor.'

'May I humbly be allowed to make one last observation?'

'Only one!'

'It's going to be awfully hard to break the habit of kissing you, Aurora.'

'OK, I'll agree to certain concessions.' Her green eyes were sparkling with amusement.

'You mean you'll dole them out when and where you see fit?'

'Luke, I'll do more. I'll kiss you goodnight and take myself home to bed.' And she suited actions to words.

But it ended quite differently from how she'd planned it. It became, once again, a sensory delight that left her trembling in his arms, more physically moved by a man than she ever remembered.

'She was right,' she said huskily, when she could cope with talking.

He drew his finger around the outline of her mouth, and studied her vivid, heart-shaped little face cupped in the curve of his elbow, and ran his fingers through her tangle of curls. 'Mae West?'

'Mmm…'

'Do you mind?'

'How could I? I didn't actually resist—I didn't resist at all.' But she licked her lips cautiously.

He smiled. 'Do you remember something else you once accused me of? Men will be men?'

She nodded after a moment.

'You were so right. That was very much a ''men will be men'' reaction. In other words, I couldn't help myself.'

'Because I was being bossy?'

He looked rueful. 'Not only that, because you're gorgeous.'

She hesitated, then slid her hands around his neck. 'So are you. Quite the nicest tiger to cross my path, in fact.' And she drew his head down, kissed him lingeringly, then slipped off the settee. 'Goodnight, sweet prince,' she said softly, but with laughter dancing in her eyes, and added, as he moved, 'No, I let myself in, I can let myself out—you get back to Newton's wife!'

The laughing look she tossed him over her shoulder as she slipped out of the room told him that she was perfectly alive to the fact that Newton's bloody wife, he thought darkly, was going to be extremely cold comfort.

He got up and walked over to the window to find himself suddenly pondering where, exactly, Aurora Templeton fitted into his scheme of things. The view over the lit pool did not vouchsafe any answers. He rubbed his jaw restlessly and contemplated the fact that, above all, he didn't seem to have a scheme of things any more.

As his father had been at pains to point out to him, he'd walked away from one woman into the arms of another—why? Not because Leonie had changed in any way, which was what was making it so hard for her to understand... He moved his shoulders restlessly and recalled that his father had even gone further and confessed that he'd almost got cold feet as the altar had approached, but his marriage to Luke's mother had been as strong and enduring as they came so if it was marriage Luke was afraid of—who was to say Aurora would be a better candidate than Leonie?

He had a point, Luke conceded to himself. Unless Aurora had read him better than any of them and he was wedded to his science?

But if that were so and all else aside, was it fair to keep pursuing Aurora? A girl, he reminded himself, who had fought almost tooth and nail to retrieve her diaries because not only had they been intimate memoirs but her mainstay in a life with no mother and a father gone a lot of the time. A girl who talked to her goldfish... And fair to keep pursuing her for no reason other than that he simply didn't seem able to help himself?

CHAPTER SEVEN

A WEEK later Aurora got to meet Leonie Murdoch.

It happened by accident, literally.

Aurora was at a junction in her car, not far from Luke's house as it happened, on her way home from work for lunch. It was a busy intersection and she was turning across the traffic. She'd been waiting a couple of minutes when the car behind her, also there for a couple of minutes, suddenly accelerated and crashed into the back of her. Fortunately her car was not propelled forward far enough to be thrust into the stream of traffic, but it was enough to give her quite a fright.

So she was fuming when she got out of her car, and more so to see the crumpled back of it with a sapphire-blue BMW nose buried in it.

'Where did you get your licence—out of a cornflake packet?' she yelled at the BMW driver, a tall, elegant woman with red hair.

'Where did you get yours?' the woman responded coldly. 'I could have driven six buses across the road by now!'

'If you were at Le Mans,' Aurora shot back, 'driving a Formula One car, but this is suburban Le Manly! So, what were you planning, you dangerous idiot? To drive over the top of me?'

'Not at all.' The other woman closed her eyes in supreme frustration. 'I'm late for a meeting, I don't have time to sit behind dawdling suburban drivers and I...well, I was concentrating on the traffic, I saw a gap I could have got through and I just put my foot down.' She shrugged her silk-clad shoulders. 'It was one of those unfortunate lapses.'

Aurora studied her. Fabulous skin, gentian-blue eyes,

116

smooth silky hair expertly cut to curve beneath her chin plus a dream outfit of a wild rice silk suit, but one very uptight, superior woman inside it, she decided. And said, 'This "unfortunate lapse", which could have been fatal, incidentally, is going to cost you and your insurance company, lady! Name and address, please?'

'Naturally,' the woman replied, and reached through the window of the BMW for her purse. 'I have full insurance so there'll be no problem at all.'

'Thank you! Your lack of apology has been noted too.' Aurora accepted a business card but didn't read it. 'Got a pen?' And when that was produced, a gold one, she wrote the registration number on the back of it and asked for the name of the insurance company. 'What happens if my car is not drivable?' she enquired then.

'For heaven's sake—let's see!'

'Your concern has also been noted, Ms—' Aurora said acidly, and flipped the card over, only to stiffen.

'Look, I am sorry but this has been a really bad day,' Leonie Murdoch said, a little wildly, 'and I do need to get going, but if your car won't go, I could call a tow truck for you on my mobile phone, and I'd be more than happy to pay compensation or whatever while it's being fixed. Could we try it now?' she asked intensely.

Aurora hesitated for a moment and looked up the hill towards her old home, only a couple of blocks away. Then she studied the card again, but all it had was a business address on it. She said, at last, in a different manner, 'OK. You reverse a bit and I'll see what happens.'

As it happened the damage to her car was only superficial and the BMW had a couple of minor dents. So when they'd established this, Aurora drew one of her cards out of her purse and handed it over. But Leonie Murdoch didn't even glance at it before they parted company.

And whether Leonie, when she'd calmed down, would associate the name of the girl she'd bumped into with her ex-lover, Luke Kirwan, Aurora had no way of knowing. But she couldn't shake the strong feeling that Luke might have contributed to Leonie's bad day. Why else would she be so close to his home—unless she lived in Manly herself? But even then—why else would she make a basic driving error of the kind she had unless she really was distraught about something?

'Neil,' Aurora said later that day, 'does Leonie Murdoch live around these parts?'

Neil blinked. 'No, she has a unit at Kangaroo Point, right on the river. Why?'

'Just wondered. How's it going with Mandy?'

Ten minutes later, she had the latest, detailed account of Neil's turbulent affair with Mandy Pearson, and Neil had forgotten about her earlier question.

But that evening, before Aurora could make up her mind whether to tell Luke about what had happened, he called to see her unexpectedly. Her car was parked in the drive because she'd been planning to go out again, and he came in with a quizzical little smile on his lips and an attitude that annoyed her and provoked her into revealing it.

'Did you reverse into something, Aurora?'

'Why would you immediately assume that?' she asked exasperatedly.

He smiled crookedly, taking in her hot pink bike shorts and tiny knit top with narrow pink and green diagonal stripes that tied behind her neck and around her waist. Her hair was gathered back with a bright green plastic grip and her feet were bare. 'Women drivers have a reputation for it.'

'I've never reversed into anything in my life! I got *run* into, as it happens, and by your ex-mistress...' She stopped and looked heavenwards.

Luke had already got his hands around her waist and they tightened unexpectedly. Aurora winced and he said immediately, 'Sorry,' and released her. 'You surprised me,' he added. 'Are you serious?'

She shrugged, 'I wasn't going to tell you, well, I don't think I was but—yes, one Leonie Murdoch, stockbroker, did drive her sapphire BMW into the back of me, although I don't think she had any idea who I was.'

He frowned. 'Why weren't you going to tell me?'

Aurora sat down on the settee and curled her legs up beneath her. 'I'm not sure, Luke.'

He stood quite still for a moment, then came to sit beside her. 'You must have some reason.'

She pulled a cushion into her arms, then raised her eyes to his. 'I could be quite wrong, but she was coming from the direction of your house—it was at that intersection just down the hill. She was in a state otherwise it would never have happened, she said as much herself, so I couldn't help wondering if you were the cause of her distraction.'

'Would this have been around lunch-time today?'

'Yes, Luke.' She hesitated. 'Another attempt to patch things up?'

He sat forward with his hands clasped between his knees. 'She came to see me with something like that on her mind, yes.'

'So it's not all over for her?'

'Aurora—' he turned his head to look at her and his eyes were sombre '—no. But there's not a lot I can do about it.'

'Except, perhaps, never having let it get to the stage it did before you decided to run for cover?'

'I didn't—' he paused '—I don't think this will blight Leonie's life, although it's obviously going to take some adjustment. Would you rather I'd married her and then conceded that it wasn't going to work?'

'How do you know that?'

He glinted her an ironic little look.

Aurora moved restlessly. 'I just…feel, I don't know. Uneasy!'

'What did you think of her?'

'Not much at first,' she said ruefully. 'I called her a dangerous idiot and asked her if she'd got her driver's licence out of a cornflake packet, but I did get a fright and she was quite…snooty. At first. Then…kind of desperate. But extremely beautiful.'

'Beauty can be in the eye of the beholder,' he observed.

'It can,' Aurora agreed tartly, 'but no beholder would quibble with her beauty!'

'I meant, I guess, beauty is not the only thing to take into consideration, nor are brains, which she has plenty of, but there are other things that count.'

'Of course.' She shrugged after a long moment. 'How are you getting on with Newton's wife?'

He blinked. 'He didn't appear to have one…'

'I know. I looked him up. His mother abandoned him to his grandmother until he was about nine, he was always cantankerous by the sound of it and had at least two nervous breakdowns. I can't find any reference to Halley having a wife, or Ptolemy, either. No one's even sure when he was born or died!'

'You have done a bit of research,' he commented. 'But Marie Curie was both a wife and a physicist.'

'Her husband was a physicist too,' she said a shade bleakly.

'Aurora, are you trying to tell me again that I'm wedded to my science? If so, may I point out that I'm in no way comparable to Newton, Galileo, Halley or any of those wifeless wonders? If, indeed, they all were. And there must be many more who weren't.'

Aurora chewed her lip. 'I think, though, I need a bit of breathing space, Luke. But more than that, I think *you* should have some.'

'Breathing space?'

She nodded. 'Three years is a long time to be cast off so…so—' she shrugged '—precipitately.'

'Only a week or so ago, you were of the opinion that we should continue to get to know each other,' he pointed out dryly.

'I hadn't bumped into the woman then, I hadn't seen her—distress,' she said intensely.

'All right.' He stood up. 'How long did you have in mind?'

Aurora stared up at him a little nervously, as, by some mysterious process, the man she'd first laid eyes on beside the piano in her old home came into play. He was nowhere near as formally dressed as on that occasion—cargo pants, a sky-blue polo shirt and trainers—and his sleeked-back hair was falling in his eyes, but all the bored arrogance she'd seen that night was suddenly back.

'Until you—I don't know,' she said helplessly.

'Do you remember walking out on me the other night?' he asked abruptly.

'I...I remember leaving you,' she said. 'Why? Did I do something wrong?'

He looked at her with a tinge of mockery. 'Yes and no. You left me to meditate on a lovely slim body, you left me with the feel of the curves of your breasts and hips beneath my hands, the silk of your skin under my fingers and the delicious taste of you on my lips—what's more you knew it, Aurora.'

'I...perhaps,' she conceded with her eyes wide and her own memories flooding her, 'but....'

'Did you—' he indicated the fish tank '—confide some thoughts on the subject to Annie and Ralph? Your diary perhaps? Or did you fall immediately into a deep and dreamless sleep?'

She got up slowly and walked towards the kitchen, feeling hot and uncomfortable all over.

He trapped her against the two-way counter that served as a breakfast bar on the lounge side. He simply rested his hands on it around her. She looked down at their lean strength on either side of her, then concentrated on a brightly painted china bowl laden with apples, oranges and grapes in a bid to control the wave of desire just the sight of his hands and the remembered feel of them on her breasts did to her. But when that little battle was over, she turned to him. 'If you must know,' she said evenly, 'I felt so good, I did just that.'

He still had her pinned against the counter, and the impact of the rest of him so close to her was even worse than the sight of his hands. His polo shirt moulded the lines of those wide shoulders and the sleek muscles beneath. She knew his chest was hard and powerful but that to nestle against it was unique for her. She knew that she loved to lay her lips on the strong column of his throat and that she sometimes felt as if she were drowning in a sea of lovely sensation when he handled her and drew her into his arms.

His gaze roamed from her serious expression to a little pulse hammering away at the base of her throat. 'Well, I didn't feel so good,' he murmured. 'I tore up three speeches, although there was nothing wrong with them. I would have given anything for a couple of goldfish to…say a few choice words to.'

She swallowed, although there was a flicker of humour in his eyes. 'I'm not sure what this is leading up to, Luke,' she said at last, 'although I apologise for inconveniencing you. It wasn't an intentional…leading-you-down-the-garden-path-then-slamming-the-door-in-your-face kind of thing. It was…' She broke off frustratedly.

'I know it wasn't deliberate. It was the pure *joie de vivre* of Aurora Templeton, it was delightful and it was my problem that it—made life a little difficult for me for a few hours. It also, surely—' he gazed down at her '—demonstrates that you're in command, Aurora.'

She raised her eyebrows. 'Why do I get the feeling that's a real trap for the unwary?'

'How so?'

'Never mind.' She looked distracted for a moment, then frowned. 'Why did you come tonight?'

'To ask you to come to the opening of the astrophysics conference.'

Her lips parted.

'Next weekend,' he went on, 'at the Mirage, on the Gold Coast. It's a dinner dance kind of thing. I thought you might like to spend the weekend down there, in your own room...' he paused as if to emphasize it '...but I guess not.'

'Luke...' she hesitated, then went on a little desperately '...don't you have any understanding of how I feel?'

He straightened and studied her. 'A sense of solidarity with your sex which countermands going to bed on the night in question *without* having to talk to your fish or your diary because you felt so good?' he suggested.

She looked exasperated, then wry, and in the end could only shrug.

He smiled slightly and traced the frown lines on her brow. 'I must tell you I don't think Leonie would reciprocate your sentiments were your positions reversed,' he remarked, however.

'Why not? I mean, that's not *all* it's about, but—' She stopped.

'Because Leonie, my dear Miss Templeton,' he said satirically, 'has no sense of solidarity with her own sex. She's fond of claiming she much prefers the company of men to women. And, in relationship to yourself, for example, she—' He broke off. 'No.'

'*What?*' Aurora insisted. 'She doesn't know me from a bar of soap—until yesterday—do you mean, she knows *about* me?' Aurora blinked several times as her mind spun. 'Through Mandy Pearson?'

'The same,' he agreed tonelessly.

'Who I've met *once*,' Aurora stated through her teeth.

Luke shrugged.

'But I know Neil a lot better,' Aurora went on as if talking to herself. 'OK,' she commanded imperiously, 'spill the beans. Leonie has obviously formed some opinion of me… Let me even guess! That you'd get bored with me in no time at all?'

For some reason he smiled briefly. 'To give her credit, she hadn't met you herself, then, so she was talking second hand.'

'All the same… Would you and Leonie have some mutual friends going to this astrophysics bash on the Coast, by any chance?'

'Aurora, yes, there may well be, but—'

'All the better,' Aurora said, with that certain glitter in her green eyes. 'So thank you for the invitation, Prof, I will come! Mind you…' She stopped and studied him suspiciously. 'Have I been set up?'

'How so?'

'I have to ask myself this—why, when only moments ago I was seriously concerned about Leonie Murdoch, am I now, following some well-planted insinuations from you, all set to give her a run for her money?'

'You can still change your mind.' His eyes laughed at her and he put his fingers beneath her chin and tilted it gently.

'Don't kiss me,' she warned. 'I'm not in the mood.'

'All right.' But he stroked her cheek.

'I don't think you should do that either,' she said after a moment. 'It's counterproductive to my state of extreme annoyance with you.'

He laughed softly. 'What can I do? How about this?' he went on before she could speak. 'In answer to your question, perhaps you've agreed to come because you can never resist a challenge? But, the real reason I asked you to this bash—' he looked rueful '—is because you're a constant source of delight to me.'

'Luke,' she whispered and licked her lips, 'am I really?'

'Believe it, Aurora.' He bent his head and kissed her very lightly.

'But I'll take no further liberties. Goodnight. I'll be in touch.'

They didn't see much of each other until the day before the conference.

Aurora was flat out herself and extremely relieved when the first session of her talk-back programme went smoothly and it got plenty of calls. Her interviewee for this occasion was an author who lived on Lamb Island in Moreton Bay and, between calls, they chatted comfortably about his tastes in music and food, his muse, as he put it, and the preservation of Moreton Bay and its islands, about which he was passionate.

The next morning a large bouquet of flowers arrived for her from Luke. The card said simply, 'Well done, Miss Sparky! Luke.'

'He listened to it,' she marvelled with the card in her hands and the flowers on her desk.

'Luke Kirwan?' Neil responded, having squinted at the card over her shoulder. 'Why wouldn't he?'

'Compared to Ptolemy, Galileo, Copernicus, Halley and Isaac Newton, not to mention stockbroking, what I do for a living is small potatoes, Neil,' she said solemnly. She waved the card. 'And this is a professor who can be—extremely scholarly and forgetful at times.'

'Didn't think that was how you saw him, Aurora,' Neil teased.

'Well, I do now. Although, that isn't all there is to him, I will concede.'

Neil laughed. 'Don't we all know it? Leonie is…in a state of contained frenzy, apparently,' he added more soberly.

'So I gather.' Aurora sighed. 'Does she know it was me she ran into?'

Neil did a double take. 'You didn't tell me that's what happened to your car!'

'I know. I just wondered whether, seeing as she and Mandy are such bosom pals, she'd connected it up.'

'Don't think so. Mandy hasn't mentioned it. Leonie would probably have just handed all the details over to her PA. It has been fixed, hasn't it?'

'Yep. Oh, well…do me a favour, Neil, and don't tell Mandy about it.'

Neil looked a little embarrassed. 'Sorry,' he said. 'I…Mandy, damn it—' he swore '—there are times when I don't know why I put up with Mandy Pearson. She's a born gossip.'

Aurora looked amused. 'But great in bed?' she suggested.

Neil looked away and the back of his neck reddened.

'Sorry,' she said, and meant it for she liked Neil, 'strike that! And getting back to these flowers…' she looked at the colourful bouquet '…it's fair to say they've made my day!'

'It's fair to say you've made mine too,' Neil responded. 'The feedback to yesterday's programme has been excellent. I've even had a request from the local paper to interview you complete with pics. Which has put me in a cleft stick.'

'Oh?' Aurora frowned at him.

He drummed his fingers on the desk. 'Only because you sound more mature than you look, Aurora. Which is not to say you look girlish but, well, you are young. Young and gorgeous. No problem with the gorgeous bit, but listeners could be surprised at how young you are.'

'Do I have any say in the matter?'

'Well—yes.' He looked at her warily, however.

Aurora grinned. 'I think I'd like to be known for my golden voice and maturity rather than my image at the moment. Let's see if it wasn't just a flash in the pan first and, anyway, a little bit of mystery goes a long way. It's one of the things I've always found so fascinating about radio, trying to put a face to the voice.'

'There, I told you you were mature, didn't I?' Neil said relievedly.

'Thanks, pal,' she laughed. 'I just wish...' She stopped and when he looked at her enquiringly, shook her head.

But later in the day, when she was home alone, she examined the thought again... I just wish Luke had the same, mature view of me...was what she'd been about to say.

Because it was impossible for her to know exactly how Luke saw her. Youthful and immature? she wondered. A girl with a core of inner loneliness—he'd got that right and he did appear to be holding back to an extent. Why?

Then it dawned on her why she was thinking these thoughts—because there was nothing immature about her feelings for Luke Kirwan. There was, instead, a conviction that she'd fallen in love with him, in fact. Why else would she love his company, and feel so lonely without it? Even when she hadn't been at all sure what kind of man he was, she reminded herself. Why else would she be starting to confide more and more intimately to her diary about him? Why else would she worry about his kids not getting an insight into his own childhood or yearn to understand him completely?

Why else was she still concerned about the way he and Leonie had parted?

All in all, it was enough to make her feel edgy, tense and heartily wishing she hadn't agreed, in a moment of madness, to the astrophysics conference. And it manifested itself when he picked her up for the drive down to the Gold Coast in the yellow Saab.

'I'm really not sure I should be doing this,' she said as she watched him place her bags in the boot.

He paused before closing the boot and looked at her searchingly.

It was four o'clock on a Friday afternoon, a clear, lovely afternoon, and the thought of a weekend with the wonderful beaches of the Gold Coast, not to mention the wonders of the Sheraton and Marina Mirage at her disposal, should have been enough to fill her with a pleasurable sense of anticipation.

Also, the hood of the Saab was down and Luke was enough to make any woman's mouth water, she thought gloomily, in light grey jeans and a charcoal shirt.

She wore a straight pale jade linen dress with dark green suede shoes. She'd had her hair cut a bit shorter so that it curled to just below shoulder-length and she had a marvellous Paisley shawl with splashes of ruby and jade to wind around her. Her make-up was light but she was perfectly groomed and deliciously perfumed.

Luke Kirwan took all this in and smiled inwardly—her expression did not quite fit with this glossy, beautifully presented Aurora Templeton who looked good enough to eat. Her beautiful green eyes were distinctly troubled.

'And here I was thinking you might be looking forward to this little break. Especially in light of all your hard work and very successful week on the airwaves! I know I am. I like your new hairstyle, by the way. Very much.' His dark eyes lingered on her shorter hair.

Aurora blinked.

He closed the boot and took her hand. 'If you don't want to come to the dinner tonight, don't—and I mean that. I can take care of myself.' He looked at her humorously. 'There's no reason why we shouldn't enjoy the weekend, though.'

She chewed her lip as she debated this with herself. 'You know that garment bag you just put into the boot?' she said at last.

'Yes. Why?'

'There's a dress inside there that I would hate to tell you the cost of, but it's the most perfect, peachy dress I think I've ever owned.'

Amusement started to gather again in his eyes. 'Go on.'

'I've never worn it, it's new and its guaranteed to slay every last astrophysicist on the planet, not to mention the

Sheraton Mirage. And last but not least anyone who might be…scouting on behalf of Leonie Murdoch.'

'So?'

She gestured. 'I just don't think I'd have the willpower, once I got there, not to don that dress and…see what happens,' she said sadly. 'In other words, I need to make a decision here and now about whether to come or not.'

'It's too late,' he said, and opened her door, still holding her hand.

'No, Luke, it's not! I—'

But he ignored her and picked her up to sit her on the bonnet of the Saab.

'Luke,' she protested, 'this is becoming a habit and, anyway, you should ask first before you manhandle me.'

'Manhandle you?' His eyes were dark and wicked.

'You know what I mean—'

'No.'

Aurora sighed. 'I'm not feeling playful, Professor,' she warned severely.

'Who said I was?' He folded his arms and contemplated her troubled expression. 'You shouldn't have mentioned the dress,' he added gravely.

Her lips parted and she narrowed her green eyes. 'Why…not?'

'I won't be able to rest until I see you in it. Does it have a Spanish flavour, by any chance?'

'No-o,' she said slowly.

'Ah. I only ask because we know all too well what happened with that outfit. Worse, this one, do you think? I just hope I'm able to concentrate on my speech, if that's the case, because—'

'Stop,' she said, trying not to laugh.

'Not until you say you'll come, Aurora.' He looked around innocently.

She did the same and saw her neighbour's lace kitchen curtain suddenly twitch closed. 'You…you're impossible!'

'I know,' he agreed. 'Especially once I've got the bit between my teeth, there's just no stopping me. I checked the weather forecast, incidentally. It's going to be a beautiful weekend on the beach. Did you pack any sensational, guaranteed-to-slay-all-the-astrophysicists-on-the-Coast bikinis, by any chance?'

'No. I need a new one. I thought I might buy one down there—oh, what the hell? Let's go, Luke.' She looked long-suffering.

'I need a bit more enthusiasm than that, I think,' he temporised.

'What you really need is not to be big enough to get your own way so frequently,' she returned bitterly. 'How did Leonie do it?'

'Stop me from getting my own way?'

'Yes!'

'She—deliberately—used certain feminine wiles that you probably would not approve of, Aurora,' he drawled.

Her lips parted and she started to colour. 'You mean…do you mean sex?'

'They generally go together, feminine wiles and sex.'

'Not—well…' Several expressions chased through her eyes, which he observed with a sense of inward laughter as he waited for what was to come, knowing that, whatever it was, it would surprise him.

It did.

Aurora slid off the bonnet unaided. 'As a matter of fact, I'm dying to go down to the Coast with you, Luke,' she said, and slipped neatly into the passenger seat.

He had to bend almost double to see her. 'I'm delighted, Aurora,' he said wryly. 'But what changed your mind?'

'Any girl who operates that way deserves what's coming to her, I guess,' she said serenely. 'I just hope you weren't concocting that because it's put me on my mettle, you see!'

'I do see and there's something irresistible about it, I must tell you.'

'Will you get in and drive this car down to the Coast?' she recommended tartly. 'I've also been known to change my mind.'

He laughed and closed her door. 'Yes, ma'am!'

The opening dinner was scheduled for eight o'clock.

That gave them plenty of time after they arrived for a lovely long walk down the beach, something they did in complete accord. Although Manly was a seaside suburb, the protected waters of Moreton Bay lapped its shores, whereas the surf beaches of the Gold Coast faced the might of the Pacific Ocean.

The air was salty as the surf pounded the beach, the sky was huge and it was all quite invigorating.

'Right,' Aurora commented as they wended their way through the beach gate, lovely gardens and around the huge pools of the Mirage resort, 'that's blown away any cobwebs and put me in the mood for the big production. Would you care to call for me at about a quarter to eight, Professor?'

'Whatever you say, Aurora.'

She cast him a suspicious look from beneath her lashes.

'What have I done now?' he enquired as they strolled along side by side.

'That meek and mild air never deceives me, Luke,' she replied. 'It generally means you're laughing at me.'

'Why would I do that?' he countered, stopping and looking down at her.

She put her head on one side. 'Because I'm a novelty?'

'You certainly are.'

She wrinkled her nose. 'Now I feel as if I should reside in a funfair.'

'Not at all—but you said it. There is another scenario that comes to mind rather than a funfair,' he added before she could respond. 'I'm sure I'd enjoy being involved in all aspects of this big production.'

Aurora opened her mouth, then closed it a little uncertainly.

'Yes,' he murmured, surveying her comprehensively in the shorts and knit top she'd donned for their walk, from her riotous hair to her bare toes. 'Were we together, we could shower together, then indulge in a glass of champagne together as we relaxed for a little while and—after that, I could help you to dress. Those kind of to-die-for dresses often need a man's hand to zip you into them and I'm quite sure I'd love to be the one to do it.'

She stared up into his eyes, then blinked a couple of times at the images running through her mind—of herself dressing in front of this man, of his hands on her bare skin, of them showering together. And it took quite an effort to say, although huskily, 'Not today, Luke.'

A shadow of a smile touched his mouth. 'Maybe not. But think about it if you're tempted to feel like a sideshow, not to mention the error of my ways. I know I will be…'

Her room had an ocean view, was beautifully appointed with wooden shutters at the windows and was spacious.

So spacious, she was able to roam around it, thinking deeply for quite a few minutes without feeling caged in. Strange sentiments, she mused. Did it mean he still thought of her as the error of his ways? Did she…? Why had she got this feeling things had come to some kind of a pass between them?

Because of the imminent confrontation with so many people who could compare her with Leonie Murdoch, she answered herself dryly.

Because she was deeply unsure in her heart of hearts of what she was doing here, and what the future held for her in relation to Luke Kirwan, she added to herself, and sat down rather suddenly on the bed, to wonder intensely—why now?

Yet it wasn't such a poser, she discovered. She knew,

even if he did not, that she was in love with him. She knew instinctively and always had that there were two sides to him, just as she knew she was engaging the lighter side of that hawk-amongst-the-sparrows persona she'd seen in him—lovely though it was for her. How long it would appeal to him was another matter, though.

She sighed, then shook out her hair and went to have a shower. It was while the water was streaming down her body that she decided she wouldn't be making any statement tonight, to anyone. Yes, she'd be there, but it would be very restrained Aurora Australis, she thought, and closed her eyes...

An hour later she was almost ready.

All that remained was to step into her dress. Her hair and make-up were perfect—the new length was lighter and easier to handle besides being essentially chic, she felt. Her lashes were carefully darkened so that her eyes were even more stunning, her lips were a glossy berry-red with her nails painted to match, and her underwear was flesh-coloured; briefs, suspender belt and the sheerest of nylons. And her skin gleamed peachy pale and satiny, anointed with a light body lotion that matched her perfume.

She picked her dress up from the bed and stepped into it. As she reached for the zip, she slid her feet into glorious high strappy sandals.

Five minutes later, after a repeated knock at her door, she went to answer it with sheer frustration written all over her face.

Despite this, Luke Kirwan in a black tuxedo with a blinding white pleated shirt-front, a hand-tied tie and silver-rimmed onyx buttons down the front of his shirt, with his hair brushed back sleekly, caused her to catch her breath.

'Aurora,' he said, skimming a dark, quizzical gaze up and down her, 'you're right, that dress is something else—but what's the matter?'

The dress was made of a very fine raspberry velvet, cut low at the back with the front gathered at the throat to a narrow neck band. From the hips, matching raspberry silk georgette was gathered to form a billowing skirt dotted with delicate gold roses. She loved the sleek, fitted feel of the bodice that also exposed her shoulders and back, then the extravagance of the skirt.

But as she held it up in front of her, she said exasperatedly, 'What's wrong? You've jinxed me once again, Luke! I can't do up the neck band!'

'Hey—' he smiled crookedly and put a fingertip on the point of her chin '—no need to get into a state. I have some experience in these matters, as I mentioned.'

She let the dress go, then grabbed the front just before it fell down to reveal her bra-less breasts. 'That's another thing I object to—how very experienced you are, Luke! I…I…' She couldn't go on as no suitable explanation came to mind, then one did and she added, 'I feel as if I'm standing in a long *line* of women you've…either dressed or undressed!'

'Aurora—' he was suddenly quite sober '—not a long line, but there have been some. Nor was I intimating anything of the kind—it's just…' he shrugged '…one of those humorous things. Turn around.'

She eyed him mutinously.

'Look,' he drawled, 'surely you would feel more comfortable continuing this debate fully dressed rather than having to clutch at yourself to remain decent—if that's how you see it? I wouldn't see it as indecent, personally, but it's up to you.'

She nearly bit her tongue as she snapped her teeth closed and swung on her heel.

He said nothing more, not even when she trembled at the feel of his cool fingers on the back of her neck. And finally the little hooks and eyes yielded to his ministrations and she was done up.

'Thank you,' she said expressionlessly over her shoulder.

He merely nodded and walked away from her to the mini-bar where he drew a half-bottle of champagne from the fridge and dislodged the foil cap. He poured two glasses and brought them over to where she was still standing.

'Take a deep breath, Aurora.'

'Why?' She reached out a hand for the glass but he withheld it from her.

'Just do it,' he ordered. 'Square your shoulders and tilt your chin.'

She hesitated, then did it all.

'Perfect,' he said softly. 'Small but regal. It is a peach of a dress, one of the nicest I've ever seen—and positively exquisite down to your fingertips. There.' He put the glass into her hand. 'Now you can tell me to go to hell if you want to.'

'Luke…' she clutched the glass, then took a sudden sip, and started to smile '…how could I after that? Thank you.'

He smiled back at her, then pushed a hand into the pocket of his trousers and studied her narrowly. 'You could tell me if it was only the dress you were so worked up about?'

'I…what else could it have been? It's lovely here.' She moved at last and went to the windows, but night had claimed the view, although she stared out at it for a moment before turning back to him.

'Deep and philosophical thoughts on the nature of life and love?' he suggested.

Her lashes fluttered, giving her away, but she wasn't ready to admit anything in the spoken word. 'Not an appropriate time to be having those, I—'

'I was,' he interrupted.

Her lips parted. 'You were?' she said barely audibly, with surprise written large in her expression. 'But you've been so…so playful today.'

He smiled unamusedly. 'All the same, it's finally come home to me that perhaps I'm not being—quite fair to you.'

'In what way?'

'I'm actually starting to feel—less playful and more and more deeply attracted to you, Aurora. But I have no idea where it might lead.'

She swallowed a lump in her throat and sipped some champagne. 'At least that's honest. I might have preferred it if you'd told me this before you brought me down here, but at least it's honest. Come to that, I don't suppose you've ever been any different, and it's something I guess I've always known...'

She paused as he moved abruptly, then she said with a wry little gesture, 'I know you think I'm a bit of a babe in the woods, but I'm not stupid and—I still don't understand—why tell me this now?' She stared at him with a frown of incomprehension.

He stared down at his glass for a long moment and the lines of his face were suddenly harsh. Then he looked up at her. 'Because it's getting harder and harder not to seduce you, Aurora.'

CHAPTER EIGHT

'WHAT makes you think I'd be so easy to seduce?'

Luke studied Aurora pointedly. From her glamorous new hairstyle to the smooth, creamy skin of her shoulders, the curves of her breasts beneath the raspberry velvet, the slim line of her figure to her toes. Then his gaze came back to rest on her vivid little face and wide green eyes with their fringe of exotic lashes. Lastly, it moved to her glossy, berry-red lips.

Aurora stirred, unable to be unmoved by this silent catalogue of what he found attractive about her. Unable to stem the rising tide of desire within—a response to his dark gaze on her, almost as if his hands were on her as well. And the knowledge that it was getting harder and harder for her not to want to be seduced with every fibre of her being.

She swallowed and moved a couple of restless steps to put her glass down on a table. Then she said abruptly, 'That still doesn't mean to say I would…succumb, Luke.'

Something flickered in his eyes—admiration, perhaps, because she'd chosen not to ignore what had flowed between them. 'No. But it mightn't stop me trying.' He shrugged. 'And despite the playfulness of today, I can see that it's beginning to loom large for you—what road we're going down. Also,' he added, looking around, 'these kind of holiday surroundings are notorious for causing people to let down their guards, which is why I felt—honour-bound, I guess, to bring it up now.'

'But none of this occurred to you before we got here?' she asked huskily.

'The only thing…' he paused '…no, not quite—but it

137

occurred to me before we got here how much I would enjoy spending this weekend with you, Aurora.'

'Then how about letting me be the guardian of your morals for this weekend, Professor?' she suggested. 'I always knew I might be the error of your ways.' She gestured with both hands. 'Nothing's changed.'

'Aurora,' he said dryly, 'I know you can never resist a challenge, but I have to point out that I gave my…morals, for want of a better word…into your keeping quite a few weeks ago.'

She looked at him expressionlessly for a long moment, then, 'Luke, do you want me to go or stay?'

'It's not as simple as that,' he replied impatiently.

'Yes, it is. You worry about yourself and allow me to do the same. But I'm not ready to sleep with you, if that's what you're asking me obliquely. So, if you can't stand the heat, you'd better get out of the kitchen.'

'You…' he started to say with supreme frustration, then began to laugh.

Aurora waited with as much cool as she could muster.

'I wasn't asking you that obliquely,' he said at last, still looking amused. 'I was merely trying to point out that things could get to a mutual stage, a point of no return because we *both* might find we can't help ourselves. But—'

'I shouldn't rely on becoming Mrs Newton at the other end of it? Who says I want to?' she answered, and wondered if a bolt of lightning might strike her down there and then.

It didn't, but her comment did sober Luke Kirwan up. 'Very well, Miss Templeton,' he said at last, after studying her intently. 'Shall we go?'

'One last thing, Luke. I'm not throwing down any gauntlets. Don't *you* suddenly start taking this up as a challenge.'

He came towards her and tilted her chin as he was so often wont to do. 'Isn't that a little like the kettle calling the pot black, Aurora?'

'No.' Her lips quivered in anticipation of one of his light, chaste kisses but it didn't come.

'Then I shall try to be on my best behaviour. Dresses like this one make it difficult, however.' He traced the bare skin of her shoulder.

She shivered but forced herself to rally. 'Point taken—I'll opt for sackcloth and tents from tomorrow, but there's nothing to be done about tonight.'

'Not a thing,' he responded gravely, and did kiss her briefly this time before presenting her his arm formally.

'Luke...' She stopped uncertainly.

He raised an eyebrow and all the dangers signals she'd ever seen in him were back.

So, despite many inward qualms, she straightened her shoulders and tilted her chin again. 'Nothing.' She put her arm through his.

He smiled, but it did nothing to reassure her because it was just about the most enigmatic smile she'd ever seen.

The ballroom at the Mirage was dimly lit and decorated in silver and gold; stars, moons and planets were suspended from a midnight-blue ceiling by invisible thread. It was like stepping into the night sky. In fact Aurora was so enchanted, she forgot to be annoyed with or intimidated by Luke for a while.

It was also a large gathering, at least five hundred guests, she surmised, which had to make it easier to be anonymous. But there was another surprise waiting for Aurora on what turned out to be a never-to-be-forgotten night. She should have expected it. There was ample evidence that Luke was very much sought out by delegates to this conference even before he made his speech.

That he alone amongst the speakers would get a standing ovation had not occurred to her, although just to see him on the dais looking so tall and distinguished wreaked a bit of havoc with her already uncertain peace of mind. But he was also a consummate speaker, entirely at ease, and she suddenly found herself feeling some sympathy for the army of groupies he had to guard against.

It was one of the cleverest speeches she'd ever heard. He got his audience in stitches as, throughout a blending of the old and new in astrophysics, he wove in Isaac Newton's imaginary and long-suffering wife in the form of plaintive asides addressed to ''Mr Newton'', as she called him, about all the trials and tribulations of living with a scientist—and her sad conclusion was that it was the apple falling on his head that had done it because he'd never been the same since.

'That was brilliant!' she said, looking at him a little wonderingly, when he finally got back to her side. 'I didn't know.'

He stared into her eyes and she could see devilry in his quite clearly. 'You suggested it.'

'But I didn't think you were going to go with it and— what I meant was—I didn't know you were so good at that kind of thing.'

'Could I have redeemed myself somewhat, Aurora?' he enquired with his lips twisting.

She laughed a bit dazedly.

'For example,' he went on, 'now all that is out of the way as well as dinner, might you consent to dancing with me?'

'I...' she looked around to see that quite a few couples had drifted onto the floor '...yes, thank you. That would— probably be nice.'

He grinned wickedly and said no more. But he gathered her slim body in its beautiful red dress close to him and, with the aid of the music, wove another kind of magic around her. The sheer magnetism and sensuality of being in his arms was impossible to resist... She even thought once, with an inward little shiver, that she was trapped and held spellbound by this man, and nothing seemed to have the power to change the fact that he was the dazzling centre of her universe.

They sat down after about half an hour and she was introduced to a number of intellectuals and academics, and formed the impression that they played as well as any other kind of people. There were also plenty of wives in evidence, although many of them laughingly commented to Luke that he'd got it so right—scientists were sheer hell to live with!

Causing Aurora to shiver again and cast a swift glance at Luke by her side. He was listening to a grey-haired, venerable-looking man who was inviting him to America to do a lecture series. Despite sounding grateful for the invitation, his reply was noncommittal…

'Don't you want to go to America?' she asked as they drifted back onto the floor.

'I love America but I'm not into lecture tours.'

'You should be—you could make a fortune, I'm sure.'

He looked down at her with clear laughter in his eyes.

'You don't need another fortune—silly me,' she murmured.

'It's not that. There are times when disseminating information goes against the grain with me.'

She blinked. 'Why?'

'Well, of course one needs universities and their research facilities and it wouldn't be fair not to pass on knowledge, but…' he paused, then went on a little dryly '…there are times when I'd like to go and live in a mud hut on the Amazon and just keep it all to myself.'

'That's not,' Aurora said bemusedly, 'the image you projected tonight, Luke.'

'I only let that guy out once or twice a year. It's not the real me.' He looked down at her in an oddly sombre way. 'And, since this has been topical between us lately, Leonie would die rather than live in a mud hut.'

She missed a step and he gathered her close, then stopped dancing abruptly as he stared over her shoulder. Aurora turned after a moment, and there was Leonie Murdoch behind her on the arm of a man who looked distinctly embarrassed.

But Leonie herself looked stunning in a strapless sequined black dress that clung to every inch of her superb figure. Her skin was lightly tanned, her hair was intricately put up, she wore diamonds in her ears and on her wrist, and her whole presence was enough to make most men, as they danced by, take a second, lingering look.

But it was the contact, almost like an electric current, between her and Luke as they exchanged glances that struck Aurora like a blow to the heart, and convinced her that, whatever there was between Luke and his ex-mistress, it wasn't over...

Then Leonie switched her gentian gaze to Aurora, and she blinked as recognition came to her. 'So,' she drawled, 'you're not only the girl who's stepped into my shoes but the girl I ran into!'

'I am the girl you ran into,' Aurora agreed, 'but I haven't stepped into anyone's shoes yet.'

The faintest smile played over Leonie Murdoch's exquisite mouth, causing Aurora to feel, amongst other things, quite insignificant. Then the other girl looked back at Luke and there was so much quizzical humour in her eyes, from feeling insignificant Aurora went to feeling like scratching Leonie's beautiful eyes out...

She was saved by the bell—in a manner of speaking. The band stopped playing and announced a short break. Aurora turned to Luke and said beneath her breath, 'Get me out of here!'

He did.

Without asking, he led her not to her room but through the gardens to the beach, then stopped frustratedly and looked down at her sandals.

'I can take them off.' She did so and put them under the

hedge. 'Don't worry about my stockings. Did you *know* she was going to be here tonight?'

'No, of course not. That was her brother she was with, incidentally. He's a lecturer in my department, that's how we met in the first place—are you all right?'

'Absolutely on top of the world—what do you *think*?' Aurora said intensely. 'I would never have come if I'd known.'

'Aurora, I did not know,' he said harshly. 'The last person I would have expected her to come with was her brother.'

'I take your point, but, if she had to fall back on her brother, how desperate must she be to get you back, Luke?'

He turned away and stared out to sea.

Aurora closed her eyes and counted to ten. Then she took his hand and they started to walk, skirting the tracery left by the tide, Aurora holding her skirt up with one hand. The moon, a full one, was heading for the western horizon behind them, but its glow was giving an other-worldly look to the beach and the surf, bright yet seen through a glass darkly.

She mentioned it.

He agreed and added, 'It's the autumn equinox tonight—the days start to get shorter, the nights get longer.'

They walked for a while in silence, then she said, 'Tell me about a mud hut on the Amazon.'

He considered, then sighed suddenly. 'That's a bit extreme, but there's a call, there always has been to places like Patagonia, the Russian steppes, the Antarctic, the Dead Sea and, closer to home, the Simpson Desert, et cetera. A call to slough off…everything for a couple of months and just do my own thing. I always assumed, with Leonie, that when the call came she'd be content to stay here and do her own thing.'

'She wouldn't have been?'

'At first it was no problem but, funnily enough, it was the closest to home call that began to create problems. This may surprise you but for a while now I've been thinking of going back to Beltrees.'

Aurora stopped walking in supreme surprise. 'To...to grow wool?'

'No. To potter for a while. Years ago I came across some evidence that suggested a meteor strike on the property. I don't know if you remember, but some months ago something fell out of the heavens?'

Aurora blinked, then nodded. 'Something about the size of a golf ball that left a huge dent in the earth?'

'Yes.' He looked amused. 'Anyway, it reactivated my interest in Beltrees from that point of view, but I was too tied up at the time to be able to do anything about it. And Leonie suggested that, since I'd always have Beltrees and any trace of meteor activity wasn't going to go away, perhaps we could fit it around a more suitable time for both of us.'

'That seems a fairly reasonable suggestion.'

'I know. I kept telling myself it was entirely sensible, in fact, but...' He stopped and sighed.

'That's when you started to feel you were looking down the barrel of a gun?' Aurora suggested.

'In hindsight, again,' he said dryly, 'yes. And, selfish as it sounds, that's when a lurking sense of... I don't want to have to fit in with anyone else's timetable'' started to rise to the surface.'

'This is not, though,' she said cautiously, 'a problem with Leonie so much as a problem with yourself.'

He stopped walking and looked down at her sardonically. 'You're determined to side with Leonie for reasons that escape me.'

'That's because you're not a woman,' she replied with a trace of her own irony. 'And I'm not saying I side with her, but that doesn't mean to say that I can't see the problem loud and clear—you don't really want a wife.'

He swore beneath his breath. 'I don't want a wife who is going to resent having to give up her career for me or feel slighted when I go away or make me feel unreasonable when I know damn well I *am* being unreasonable but I can't…help it. The other thing is, Leonie thought she had a tame professor in tow, and that life would be…like this.' He looked around. 'Plenty of social intercourse—'

'She must be very naïve, which I doubt,' Aurora broke in to observe, 'if she ever thought you were "tame".'

He shrugged. 'I meant from the point of view that, while she tried to be all sweet reason at times, she thought she was humouring me. She didn't really understand…what drives me and always will.' He made a frustrated gesture. 'But I'm extremely regretful on her behalf that it took me so long to work it all out.'

They were standing facing each other on that long silvery strip of sand with the lights of Surfers Paradise pricking the dark sky and the waves beside them showing fascinating glimpses of phosphorus glowing as they curled over.

He could probably explain that phenomenon to me, Aurora thought as she stared past him out to sea, and I'd love him to do so. Why don't I just ignore all the rest of it, all the tortured complexities of his relationship with Leonie, all the things that would make any relationship with a woman difficult for him and…deadly for her if she wanted to make it permanent?

Because I can't guarantee I could stand it any better than Leonie Murdoch, she thought with chilling clarity. I can't guarantee that at all…

'Luke—' she moved her hand in his '—let's go back. I'm getting tired of holding my skirt up, for one thing!'

He looked down at her intently, then shrugged. But at the beach gate there was a bench and she sat down on it with her sandals in her hand. He stood in front of her with his hands shoved into his pockets, tall and dark.

'I'm going home first thing tomorrow morning, Luke,' she said quietly, gazing up at him and hoping desperately she was able to contain the tears that were threatening. 'Please don't say anything to try to make me change my mind. It's not Leonie, it's me. You were right when you said earlier that things could get out of hand down here—actually, I think we've got to a stage where things could get out of hand anywhere. But I'm not ready to take that step. I took it once with disastrous consequences, well—' she gestured and her sandals fell onto the sand '—that's how it seemed at the time, anyway.'

He bent down to pick them up and put them on the bench beside her. 'Are you suggesting I'd go all jealous and possessive on you?'

'No.' A stray tear did fall as she smiled at the irony of that, and licked it from her lip. 'The opposite, if anything, but just as bad, I guess—*I* might.'

'Aurora—'

'Luke—' she leant forward and rested her head on his waist '—I'd hate it if you became the error of *my* ways, but that's what it could easily become because I know very well I could be making a mistake. I like you too much for that and I think, in your heart of hearts, you might feel the same.'

He said nothing for a long time, although he started to stroke her hair. 'If,' he said at last, 'I agree with you, it's only because…I would hate to hurt you, Aurora.'

'I know,' she said huskily. 'And I thank you. Look…' she tilted her head to see his eyes '…this is difficult, but I'm sure it's for the best for both of us. Will you let me just get myself home tomorrow? They could arrange a car for me.'

His fingers slid down the curve of her cheek. 'If it gets too difficult, I—'

'No, Luke.' She stood up with her throat working but no tears in her eyes now. 'I know what I'm doing and there's no point in dragging it out. I'll be fine.' Her lips curved into the faintest smile. 'It all started with my diaries; that's where it will end.'

'And when you're an old lady with grandchildren at your

feet, you might read them over and smile a sort of smile no one will understand?' he suggested roughly.

'Maybe—but I'll still know I did the right thing. Goodbye…'

He said her name and caught her wrist. But she kissed his fingers then looked up at him steadily. And the pressure on her wrist relaxed gradually until he released her. 'Goodbye,' he said, with an effort. 'Don't go invading people's houses or doing anything crazy.'

'I won't,' she promised. 'You look after yourself too.' She picked up her sandals and slipped away from him through the gate.

He stared after her until all he could see were the little gold roses of her skirt and the pale skin of her back picking up the reflected glow of the flares that lit the path, then nothing. And he turned towards the sea and told himself it *was* for the best. He'd been a fool to let it get this far anyway; she'd be much better off without him…

So why did he have the feeling he'd let something rare and more valuable than rubies and pearls slip through his fingers like an exquisite butterfly?

CHAPTER NINE

ABOUT two months later Jack Barnard was having dinner with Luke Kirwan at the house on the hill.

Summer had slid into a so far mild winter and they were able to eat outside on the terrace with the night view spread beneath their feet. Chinese take-away was what they were indulging in, with a fine bottle of chardonnay. Jack had brought the wine in anticipation of one of Miss Hillier's delicious concoctions that she often left for Luke to warm up; Luke had rung up for the food after explaining that Miss Hillier was on holiday for a week.

'How on earth will you cope?' Jack asked of his friend. 'I may not like the woman, but in most respects she's a gem. Fancy finding a secretary who also cooks!'

Luke looked at him wryly. 'I can cook some basics when I feel like it, Jack. I'm not completely useless.'

'Never said you were.' Jack partook of the delicious sweet and sour pork. 'But you must admit she runs things down to the smallest detail. Is that why you're off to Beltrees for a while?'

Luke lifted his glass and studied the golden green contents. 'Not necessarily. Barry and Julia are off overseas for a couple of months and my father needs a hand. I also want to search for meteorite fragments.'

'This wouldn't have anything to do with the fact that Leonie has been seen out and about with a new man?' Jack enquired.

Luke grimaced. 'Has she? I didn't know.'

'Question answered,' Jack murmured. 'Are you at all interested?'

'I'm quite sure you're going to tell me whether I am or not.' Luke regarded his friend quizzically.

'A media magnate, twice divorced but very wealthy. Something of a playboy, I gather. Of course we're all wondering whether it's designed to make you jealous, but you don't seem to be in circulation much these days—by the way, I believe you've put this house on the market?'

Luke looked around. 'Yes,' he said pensively.

'Why? Because of Leonie?'

'Not because of Leonie. I've never felt the same about it since I…suffered a home invasion one night.'

Jack blinked through his glasses. 'You never told me that!'

'Probably because I came out of it looking a bit of a fool. I left the front door open, not that sh—' He stopped. 'And I actually got knocked out briefly in the encounter. Nothing was stolen, though.'

'Well, I don't blame you in that case, but…' Jack paused '…it's a funny thing—the bloke you bought it from has gone missing. I remembered the name because I did the conveyancing and I don't think there'd be too many Ambrose Templetons around—what's the matter?'

'Gone missing how?'

'Um…he was sailing round the world single-handed but he seems to have disappeared somewhere between the Cook Islands and Tahiti. I heard it on the news this morning—Luke, I didn't think you ever met him, but you look quite strange!'

'I'm sorry about this, Jack, but I have to go out… Please finish your dinner, though, and if you wouldn't mind locking up for me when you leave—there's a Yale on the front door now, you just have to pull it closed.'

'Well—' Jack half rose as Luke Kirwan was about to step inside '—I…I…'

'I'll call you, Jack!' He disappeared. Two minutes later the Saab, parked in the driveway, roared to life.

Jack sat back and sipped his wine dazedly. 'He hasn't been the same since he bought this damn house,' he commented to himself. 'I'd love to know what the hell is going on!'

Aurora was at home alone, huddled on her settee, staring at her fish.

She heard the knock and her heart started to race—news, surely! But in her haste to get to the door she tripped on the edge of a rug, and she must have left the door unlocked anyway because it opened before she got there—and Luke was standing in her hall.

She stared at him wordlessly as if he were an apparition, then, when he came to her and put his arms around her, all her pent-up emotion burst the banks she'd so rigidly erected and she collapsed against him with her eyes streaming and sobs shaking her.

Five minutes later she was sitting on his lap on the settee and taking sips of brandy from the glass he held for her. Nor did he allow her to speak until she'd finished the small tot and stopped shuddering.

He put the glass on the elephant table and eased her more comfortably against him. 'Tell me what happened?'

She sighed desolately. 'No one knows. He'd arranged a regular sked—radio schedule with an HF station in New Zealand that was also to be relayed here to Manly, and he called me once a week on his satellite phone. But the call is five days overdue now and no one's been able to raise him by radio.'

'That doesn't mean—'

'I know,' she broke in intensely, 'I know it all. It could just be battery problems; radios, phones, they all need some kind of power and he did have a hiccup with the phone about a month ago. But he does have a solar pack on board... He also has an EPIRB, an emergency position indicating radio beacon, that is...'

'I know how they work,' Luke said quietly. 'So no signal's been picked up?'

'No. Which either means he hasn't had to use it or...' she swallowed '...he went down before he could use it. There are so many things...whales, containers, storms.' She stopped helplessly.

'Has a search been mounted?'

'Yes,' she whispered. 'I wanted to go but they said wait a while. They don't really know where to start.'

'I'm not into boats myself, but Barry and Julia are, as you know, and one of their favourite catch cries is when one thing goes wrong you can bet your bottom dollar it won't be the only one, so it could well be batteries, or loose wires in a radio and another hiccup with the phone.'

Aurora smiled shakily. 'I've worked at the Coastguard long enough not to be amazed at all the things that can go wrong on boats, but this is different. It's not only my father—it's the South Pacific out there, not Moreton Bay.'

'Of course,' he said quietly and frowned. 'Why are you here on your own?'

'I...I wanted to be,' she whispered.

'Or because there's no one close enough to care?' he suggested.

She shook her head. 'It's not that. I've got friends, colleagues, mates at the Coastguard, they've all been so wonderful, but...' She stopped and sighed. 'I just wanted to be alone.'

He moved, but her eyes widened and her hands clenched. Damp tendrils of hair were clinging to her face from the storm of tears and he studied that little face, thinking it seemed to have fined down so her green eyes were even more stunning with their wet lashes sticking together in clumps. She wore a lightweight track suit the colour of lemon grass with green sand shoes but he could feel the fine, delicate lines of her body beneath it. Her heavy hair had grown again and was tied back loosely.

'I…was going to suggest,' he said slowly, 'that I made us some of your Arusha coffee—have you eaten lately?'

'No, but coffee would be lovely.'

'Have you got any bread and cheese?'

'Um—yes but—'

'Do you like toasted cheese?' he interrupted.

'Luke—' she paused '—can you make toasted cheese?'

'I don't know why everyone assumes I'm quite useless,' he remarked bitterly. 'I make the best toasted cheese this side of the black stump!'

'Who else has been trying to make you feel useless?' she queried with a smile trembling on her lips.

'My friend Jack Barnard,' he explained. 'That's how I heard about your father. Jack heard it on the radio and remembered the name because he did the conveyancing on the house. In fact Jack, for all I know, is still sitting on the terrace finishing off the Chinese dinner.'

'Thank you for rushing over,' she said softly. 'And, yes, I do like toasted cheese.'

Half an hour later, she'd finished her toasted cheese and was inhaling the delicious aroma of the Arusha coffee. Luke had pulled up an armchair to the coffee-table and was sitting opposite her.

'Tell me about your experiences of Arusha?' he invited. 'You said you'd been there.'

Aurora laid her head back. 'Ah, Arusha. Yes, my father was captaining a freighter that took a few passengers. There was stuff to be unloaded at Dar-es-Salaam and when something went wrong with the freezers on board we had about a week to kill so we hired a Land Rover and drove up.' She smiled. 'I'll never forget the mad traffic or the state of the roads in Dar. Then this good, long straight highway up country and as we got closer to Moshe we started to look for Kilimanjaro.' She stopped and her eyes were far away.

'It's quite a sight, when it reveals itself,' he commented.

'I couldn't believe it. We were looking too low, then I just happened to look up and there was this snow-clad peak rising out of a blue horizon way up in the sky. I'll never forget it.' She looked across at Luke. 'And Arusha,' she said affectionately. 'We stayed at this lovely place called Mountain Village, it's in the middle of a coffee plantation on Lake Duluti—you could see Kili from there too, as well as Mount Meru. It looked really mysterious. And we went to Ngorongoro, the Serengeti—I did a balloon safari over the Serengeti at dawn.'

'So did I. And I stayed at Mountain Village, saw the lions of Ngorongoro, the wildebeest migration across the plains of the Serengeti to the Masai Mara, saw Olduvai Gorge—in fact I climbed Kilimanjaro.'

Aurora sat up, her eyes wide and wondering. 'Oh! Tell me about it! I wanted to but we didn't have the time.'

Two hours later, they'd shared not only Tanzania but many travel experiences and Aurora was feeling more re-laxed than she had for days, even sleepy. She yawned, then apologized. 'It's not that I'm bored, but I haven't had much sleep lately.

His eyes softened. 'Why don't you go to bed?' He stood up.

She hesitated and he saw some of the ghosts come back to her eyes.

'I could stay if you liked. I could doss down there.' He nodded at the settee. 'Just give me a pillow and a rug.'

'That's very kind but—' she began.

'I wouldn't be tempted to take advantage of you,' he said quietly.

Aurora coloured. 'I didn't mean that.'

He looked at her with a sombre question in his eyes.

She swallowed. 'It's just come rushing back to me that we…well—'

'Broke up before we'd barely started?' he suggested.

If only that were true or you knew how tough these two

months have been, Luke, she thought, with her lashes lowered so her eyes were hidden from him.

Then he moved abruptly and her lashes flew up to see that the sombreness had been replaced by a slight smile as he said, 'But we did like each other, didn't we, Aurora? And that's what friends are for at times like these. So don't bother your head with all sorts of complications that don't exist. Just...' he paused, then said humorously '...throw me down a pillow and a rug and go to bed.'

After she'd done that, Aurora took a shower, donned her pyjamas and curled up in her bed with a spare pillow in her arms. She knew she should be thinking of her father—she was, but she was also thinking about Luke; she couldn't help herself. And thinking specifically about what regrets he might have—was that why he'd come? Why he'd said something about breaking up before they'd barely started? Or was he only being a good friend in need?

In which case, how much harder was it going to be for her after two months of still being sure she'd been right to walk away from him but finding absolutely no comfort in it? Despite her flourishing career—she'd made a hit on the airwaves and now had a devoted band of listeners to her talk-back session—she'd felt incredibly lost and lonely. Despite her friends and colleagues and filling her life with interests—she was rarely home—despite it all, the pain of not having Luke in her life was still with her. And now this...

Just the sight of him in khaki moleskins and a blue linen shirt she remembered well, the feel of his arms around her, the way she could talk to him was enough to...what? she mused.

Wonder if it would ever go away, that bereft feeling? Wonder how she could possibly be worse off as Newton's mistress even if she couldn't aspire to be his wife?

Her tired, overwrought mind gave up at this stage and she fell into a deep, dreamless sleep. So deep, she didn't hear the phone ringing downstairs and had no idea she'd forgotten to bring her remote phone upstairs with her.

It was his hand on her shoulder that woke her finally. She sat up brushing her hair out of her eyes and blinking like an owl. 'Who...*Luke*...what?'

He put the phone into her hand. 'Your father.'

She tensed convulsively but Luke smiled at her. 'Talk to him.'

She put the phone to her ear. 'Dad? Is that you? *Dad!*'

Twenty minutes later she ended the call and lay back against the pillows. 'I can't believe it,' she whispered, then sat up jubilantly. 'He's quite OK. It was a battery problem! Well, batteries, bilges and a storm that blew him off course—it was a long story and a bit hard to take in,' she said ruefully. 'And the satellite phone just gave up the ghost! Would you believe it?'

He sat down on the side of the bed and said gently, 'I would. And I'm so very happy for you, Aurora.'

She burst into tears.

He took her in his arms. 'I'm so happy myself,' she wept. 'I really thought I'd lost him. He managed to signal a passing freighter eventually and they came to his rescue. They let him use their equipment and he reckons he'll be able to sail back to the Rarotonga.'

'And you're going to fly over tomorrow if you can arrange it and be there on the dock to meet him.'

'Yes! Perhaps I can even persuade him to give up this round-the-world idea, but, anyway, I can at least spend some time with him. I've got some leave coming up. With a bit of juggling I can get away early.'

He brushed her wet cheeks with his fingers and cupped her face in his hands. 'I've missed doing this.'

She stared up into his dark eyes. 'I've missed it too...'

He smiled briefly. 'I never did get to kiss you goodbye.'

'Is…is that what you're going to do now?'

'Just between friends, Aurora.'

The next day she was winging her way to Rarotonga via New Zealand where she had a joyful reunion with her father but was unable to talk him out of his round-the-world voyage. It was one of the subjects they discussed in their last conversation on board the *Aurora*, before she flew back home a week later.

'I know you worry, I know the last little contretemps took its toll,' Ambrose Templeton said, 'but I'm only sixty, Aurora, and retirement, sitting at home wondering what to do with myself, frightened the life out of me. Also, I'm a sailor at heart and I've dreamt of doing this all my life. Would you, could you be generous enough to allow me to continue with my dream?'

She regarded him wistfully. He looked wonderfully well, tanned and fit, keen-eyed and not the least deterred by his brush with fate. 'Of course,' she said with a sigh. 'Just try to minimize the frights you give me!'

Ambrose hesitated. 'Are you OK?'

'Fine! Why?'

'I…I don't know, can't quite put my finger on it, but it's just occurred to me you're not quite the same. Could there be something—some reason you need me home, darling?'

'None at all,' Aurora reassured him with a grin. 'I'm probably still a bit shell-shocked, that's all. But I would hate the thought of you sitting at home twiddling your thumbs and, although I got such a fright, in my heart of hearts I know you're a consummate sailor. So you have my blessing.' She leant across and kissed his cheek.

An hour later he put her on the plane that took her home. Luke was at the airport to meet her.

She stopped as if she'd been shot as soon as she saw him.

He was wearing the same clothes as he had the first time

she'd ever seen him. Indigo jeans, a navy jacket, dark blue shirt, although today it was open at the neck.

'This...this wasn't what we decided, Luke,' she said barely audibly as he came up to her and took her bag from her nerveless fingers.

He looked down at her with a glint of mockery plain to be seen in his dark eyes. 'I didn't decide anything, Aurora. I merely went along with your bossiness because it wasn't the time or place to take issue with you.'

'Bossiness?' she repeated blankly. 'How can you *say* that?'

'What else would you call it?' he enquired. 'You chose to sleep with me, you even did it ecstatically.' He looked down her slender figure in a long straight charcoal cashmere skirt with a matching tunic top, red patent shoes on her feet and a scarlet scrunchie holding her hair back, then raised a wry eyebrow. 'You were wonderful in bed, Aurora,' he said *quite* audibly. 'Like a lovely, delicate nymph, all ivory and rose—'

'Stop it, Luke!' she whispered, looking around and nearly dying to see that several people had tuned in with various expressions of amusement or surprise.

'Only if you accept my lift home.'

'No! I...'

'All right. Do you remember when we got to a certain stage how we stopped and sang the Skye Boat song and then—'

'Where's your car?' she said wildly. 'I'll *never* forgive you for this!'

'We'll see. This way.'

She didn't say any more until she was installed in the Saab with the roof closed. Then she turned her furious green gaze on him. 'That was unbelievable! How could you?'

His long fingers played with the keys but he didn't switch the engine on. 'To tell you the truth, Aurora, I found it unbelievable you could sleep with me the way you did then issue a stilted little statement to the effect that nothing had changed and we should regard it as a ''ships passing in the night'' experience.' He looked at her dryly.

'Why…why didn't you say so at the time?' she stammered.

'You were flying out to Rarotonga the next day. You hadn't recovered from thinking you'd lost your father. You were on an emotional roundabout, that's why.'

She wet her lips. 'But nothing has changed…'

'Apart from the obvious—how would you know?' he shot back.

Several moments later when she hadn't replied, he did switch the engine on and they drove off in silence.

It was a twenty-minute drive home from the airport as darkness fell and that silence lay like a brick wall between them as Aurora recalled so many details of their lovemaking a week ago—including breaking into spontaneous song at one point because she'd felt so very good on all fronts, and her father's safety had still been on her mind, thus the Skye Boat song… She flinched inwardly.

It was she who broke the silence at last, but only to say, 'You took the wrong turning.'

'No, I didn't. You can come and have dinner with me tonight.'

'Luke…'

'Why don't you liken it to your initial experience of me?' he suggested.

'What do you mean?'

'Well, you told me you felt so frustrated you decided to take things into your own hands and it was my fault you felt that way—over the matter of getting your diaries back, Aurora,' he elucidated with an undercurrent of sarcasm.

She cleared her throat. 'I see,' she said in a voice devoid of all expression. 'All right. Just don't count on anything else happening, Luke.'

'You mean you don't see yourself as issuing any invitations tonight, Miss Templeton?'

She gasped, then said fiercely, 'We both got carried away! We...' She broke off frustratedly.

'So we did,' he drawled and drove into his driveway. 'Surely—' he cut the engine and switched his dark gaze to her '—that begs a question if nothing else?'

They ate inside; it was too chilly for the terrace.

It was all prepared and just needed heating up—lasagne and a salad, but it was delicious and bore all the hallmarks of being one of Miss Hillier's concoctions.

'I thought she was away on holiday,' Aurora remarked as they sat opposite each other across a round table in the den, where, as had been in her day, there were some deep, comfortable chairs, a television and this table for informal meals. The chairs were covered in apricot linen with navy piping, the walls were a matt wheat colour with white trim, and the curved window that looked out over the garden gave the room a conservatory feel. There was an extremely fine collection of water-colour landscapes on the walls and a wonderful bowl of gerberas from white to yellow to apricot, orange and deep pink on the coffee-table.

It wasn't an essentially masculine room, but he'd told her that he'd left most of the decorating of the house to Miss Hillier. Aurora had had the feeling ever since that Miss Hillier might have indulged herself in this one room.

Luke had not required any conversation from her until he'd served up dinner. He'd made her a drink and switched on the television so she could watch the evening news. When dinner was on the table, he switched the television off and put Vivaldi on the CD player.

'She was,' he said. 'She came back today. How did you find your father?'

Aurora told him. 'He's having the time of his life and I didn't have the heart to make a fuss,' she finished.

'Did you tell him about me?'

She lifted her gaze to his with a forkful of lasagne halfway to her mouth. 'No. There was nothing to tell.' She ate the mouthful but found it hard to swallow.

'Nothing?' He lay back in his chair and watched her idly until she started to colour.

'Luke—'

'Did it make it into your diary, Aurora? To read over when you're an old lady and—wonder what might have been if you hadn't been so stubborn.'

She stopped eating and sipped her wine. 'No, it didn't.'

'Too painful?' he suggested. 'Too many regrets, perhaps, but you don't know how to handle things since you were the one who laid down the law?'

She looked away with her cheeks now burning and wishing she could press the cool of her wineglass to them. 'Why are you doing this?' she said huskily.

'Because I'm contemplating asking you to marry me and I thought the passage of a week might have made you see things differently. If you've been able to forget that wonderful lovemaking as if it never happened, I haven't. Nor did I think you were the kind of girl to whom those things were…easy come, easy go,' he murmured with a satirical little gesture. 'Do you often sing songs in the middle of sex?'

Aurora pushed her plate away and stood up. 'If your real reason for bringing me here was to insult me, Luke, you've succeeded! Don't bother to see me out, I'll get myself home.'

'Sit down, Aurora,' he ordered.

'You can't make me!'

'I can and I will—and this time I'm serious about it,' he added with a certain rough impatience that left her in no doubt he was.

He watched her react to this, saw the way her fingers whitened on the back of the chair, and suddenly could have kicked himself. 'Please, Aurora,' he said quietly. 'I know you're trying to do what you perceive as the right thing for us, but we need to talk.'

She hesitated, then sank down in her chair.

'We don't need to make such terribly heavy weather of it, however,' he added with a faint smile. 'Tell me about Rarotonga—I've never been there.'

Aurora spread her napkin on her lap and picked up her fork. 'I can't tell you that much about Rarotonga because...' she blinked '...I could have been anywhere in the world.' She dropped her fork and put her fingers to her eyes. 'But it still wouldn't work, Luke.'

'I've done it again,' she said helplessly.

'And just as beautifully,' he agreed as he ran his fingers through her dishevelled hair. 'Mind you, we didn't sing sea shanties this time, but you have a way of making love to me that's—I don't know how to describe it, but it's like capturing a will-o'-the-wisp, a gossamer spirit, the soul of a butterfly in the guise of an exquisite girl.'

She smiled against his chest. 'Thanks, but—how fanciful is that, Professor?'

'It's true.' He drew his long fingers down her spine, then cupped her hip. 'Sleepy?'

'Yes,' she murmured.

'Be my guest.' He drew her head onto his shoulder and pulled the covers over them.

Aurora relaxed with a sigh, revelling in the warmth and the closeness, as well as the feeling of security. Five minutes later she was asleep. And the next morning she flew to Beltrees with Luke Kirwan to spend the second week of her holiday with him.

They had the house to themselves for the first four days. Sir David had taken advantage of Luke's arrival to have some time off—and this time there was no question of separate rooms.

On their first night, after a delicious dinner prepared by the housekeeper and some time spent in front of the huge log fire in the lounge, Luke led her to a double bedroom with a vast bed and its own fireplace with a three piece chintz-covered suite in front of the fire.

He didn't turn any lights on but undressed her slowly in front of the flickering flames.

'Very romantic,' she commented as he unbuttoned her blouse.

'Very,' he agreed, 'but also warm. Just think what it's like outside, clear with a million stars but distinctly cold.'

Aurora shivered. 'I'm glad I'm not out there.'

He removed her blouse, then her bra.

'Would you like me to stand on a footstool, seeing as there's no bonnet of a car handy?' she murmured mischievously.

He cupped her shoulders in his palms and stared down at her high, small breasts. 'I think I can manage. Do I—' he lifted his dark gaze to her eyes '—detect a spirit of playfulness in you, Ms Templeton?'

'Not at all, Professor Kirwan,' she denied. 'I wouldn't presume to mar the solemnity of the moment in any way.'

'Oh, yes, you would, Aurora.' He slid his hands down her arms and stroked her nipples. 'In fact, I get the feeling you specialize in a brand of lovemaking that's far from solemn.'

Her lips twitched. 'I don't happen to be a specialist at it, Professor. I just do, and say, what feels right.'

'So…' he looked down at her nipples as they started to unfurl beneath his thumbs '…at this point in time it feels right for you to point out that I could get a crick in my neck? Is that all you've got on your mind at the moment?' Once again that dark gaze sought hers.

'Not entirely,' Aurora said airily as a tremor ran through her. 'It would be fair to say my mind is on other things as well. Do you know what that does to me?'

'This?' He stroked her nipples again.

Aurora took a breath, but said very gravely, 'It's so nice I'm not sure I could stand what's still to come. It also,' she continued as he started to smile, 'doesn't seem quite fair that I should be the only recipient of this kind of…heaven.'

His smile grew. 'What would you like to do about it?'

'Oh—help you out of your clothes and—show you a thing or two, Luke Kirwan. That's all.'

'All? I don't think *I* could stand that,' he said frankly.

'Well, I think you could stand a lot more than I could,' she replied just as frankly.

'What makes you say that?' he asked curiously.

She stood on her toes and kissed him lightly. 'I just get the feeling I'm in the hands of a master. For your information, I have never sung during sex, before it or after it. And last night I went from vowing to hate you for the rest of my life to—well, being the proverbial putty in your hands.'

'There was no resemblance to putty,' he said softly. 'You were gorgeous.' His hands roamed her upper body at will.

'I think you'd better lead on,' she teased, 'before I die here on the spot.'

But later she wasn't able to tease or be playful as he drew a response from her that left her shuddering with rapture in his arms.

They had a cup of tea and toast very early next morning, then went for a ride.

Aurora wasn't that experienced with horses, but the one Luke chose for her was sure-footed and easy to handle. And he led her to an old opal mine on the property, not much more than a hole in the ground beside a mound of pebbles.

When they dismounted, Aurora looked around at the early morning sky streaked with pink and the vast red-soil country dotted with low sage-green bush that was, apparently, favourite fare for sheep. 'Wow.' She pulled off her hat, threw it into the air and swung her arms joyfully. 'This is wonderful. This is real Australia!'

He laughed. 'You're actually looking quite wonderful yourself, Aurora.'

'Ah, well, I think I might know who to thank for that!'

'I'm feeling exceptionally well myself, as it happens,' he said whimsically. 'But I happen to know exactly who to thank for it.' He reached for her and kissed her. 'You.'

She looked into his eyes and was shaken by the memories of their lovemaking. 'I...' she hesitated '...I felt as if I was flying to the moon.'

'Now who's being fanciful?' he teased. 'But I couldn't fly you to the moon unless it was something we did to each other.'

I'm not so sure about that, Aurora thought, but decided against putting it into words because she didn't think she could explain adequately...

'What is going through those beautiful green eyes at this moment, Ms Templeton?' he enquired.

'Uh—are we looking for opals or meteorite fragments, Mr Newton?' she enquired, with her hands on her hips.

He frowned faintly as if aware of the evasion, then, 'Both. But watch your step,' he warned. 'Those mounds of pebbles are extremely slippery.'

'Romeo!' she responded, causing him to raise an eyebrow at her.

'Mariner's speak,' she explained. 'In the nautical alphabet Romeo stands for R and also means "yes, will do"!'

'I gather you're an expert on mariner's speak?'

'Oh, yes. Your name would be spelled out—lima, uniform, kilo, echo...and mine is alpha, uniform, romeo, oscar, romeo, alpha—for example.'

He smiled at her crookedly. 'I've often meant to ask you why you volunteer your services to the Coastguard, alpha, uniform, romeo, oscar, romeo, alpha.'

'You picked that up pretty quickly, Professor! Um...I've always been fascinated by radio, I don't really know why. I suppose my father had something to do with it—it's such an integral part of boating. Whenever I was on board with him, I used to spend hours listening to the HF radio. Yachts talking to each other from so far away, weather skeds and the like. Then he suggested I get a radio operator's licence— anyone can take the course, so I took it at the Coastguard and enjoyed it so much I decided to volunteer—what's wrong?'

'I was just thinking…' he paused and ruffled his dark hair, looking momentarily frustrated '…that you're like no one else I know.'

Aurora eyed him in his bush shirt, khaki trousers and boots. 'I should hope so, but I don't see what's so unusual about that.'

'It's not only that. You just…continually surprise me. OK, you look for opals, I'll look for meteorite fragments.'

'I don't like to display my ignorance,' Aurora said, 'but would I know a rough opal if I found one?'

He grinned. 'Probably not. I'll show you what to look for.'

They spent a couple of hours searching and he actually found a small milky-blue opal for her. Then they rode back to the homestead like the wind and tucked into a huge breakfast. And the next couple of days were spent in similar fashion. Out and about exploring or helping work the sheep during the day and spending the nights together.

It was exhilarating by day and Aurora's skin started to glow pale gold, her green eyes shone and she knew she not only looked full of health and vitality but felt it, even in spite of some saddle stiffness she suffered. She also got extremely interested in the subject of meteorites and became as keen as Luke was for the subject.

By night, they talked, listened to music, read—he even got out his old crystal radio set and started to repair it. And they made love whenever the mood took them…

Such as the evening she looked up from her book to see him staring at her with a frown.

'Luke?' she said huskily. 'Have I done something wrong?'

He shook his head and continued to study her.

She'd changed for dinner into her charcoal cashmere skirt and tunic top—the same outfit she'd had on when he'd met her at the airport, even to her red shoes and scarlet scrunchie. They were sitting in front of the fire in their bedroom.

'What is it, then?' she asked.

The firelight played on his dark hair and those fascinating hollows beneath his cheekbones. He'd also freshened up and wore clean jeans and a thin green jumper. 'I was just wondering how to ask you to take your clothes off here and now.'

She raised a wry eyebrow. 'Is that all? You had me worried for a moment.'

'It's not that simple at all. I've been sitting here for the last ten minutes asking myself how you could serenely go on reading your book while I was beset by these fantasies.'

She closed her book and put it aside with a faint, wise little smile curving her lips. 'Who's to say I was so serene?'

'You…weren't?'

'I've just read the same page six times and didn't make any sense of it once.'

'Aurora…' He grimaced. 'I wouldn't have known.'

'That's because I didn't want you to know, just in case our minds weren't running along the same lines. But if they are…' She shrugged and stood up.

Beneath her charcoal top she wore a black bra dotted with tiny strawberries, and when she stepped out of her skirt it was to reveal matching briefs. She heard Luke take an unsteady breath as she straightened, released her hair and shook it out. Then, with her skin touched with the glow of the fire, she took her bra off and slid her briefs down. And she stood before him with her hand outstretched.

He studied the lovely curves of her body, all the slim, petite length of her, then he said rather harshly as his gaze clashed with hers, 'I might not be able to take my time over this.'

'I might not want you to,' she replied barely audibly.

'All the same...' He stopped abruptly.

'Luke, I can cope,' she said gently. 'I'm not breakable. I can even help. Take my hand.'

He got up slowly and put his hand in hers.

She raised it to her mouth and kissed it. 'Come, sweet prince, let's go to bed.'

He hesitated a moment longer, then swept her into his arms and buried his head in her hair.

When she woke the next morning, it was to see that Luke was still fast asleep. She moved cautiously, then sighed voluptuously and stared at the old-fashioned, pressed iron, intricately designed ceiling with a feeling of extreme satisfaction. Not only because of how thoroughly and marvellously sated she felt, but because, for the first time, she had been the one to bestow the fulfilment Luke had been desperate for.

It made her feel like the cat that had got the cream, she reflected ruefully. It made her feel an equal now, rather than a pupil in the hands of a master; it made her feel as if she might have taken him to the moon—instead of the other way around.

Then he stirred, sat up, running his fingers through his hair, and turned to her with sudden, obvious concern. 'How...Aurora? Are you OK?'

'Fine, Luke,' she said complacently. 'Quite fine!'

He threw back the blankets and sheet and examined her minutely.

'Luke,' she protested. 'It's cold!'

He ran his hands down her body, then pulled the covers

up so they were buried beneath them to their chins. 'Thank heavens. I thought I might have been a bit heavy-handed.'

'You were awesome.'

He gathered her close and breathed deeply. 'I certainly got a bit carried away.'

She kissed him lightly. 'It would be fair to say I loved it.'

He smiled at her. 'Sure?'

'Oh, yes,' she said a little dreamily. 'I was thinking only moments ago that I felt like the cat who got the cream. Positively smug, Professor!'

This time he laughed. 'Then how about agreeing to marry me, Aurora?'

Her expression changed slowly. 'I…' she said uncertainly, '…I don't know about that, Luke.'

CHAPTER TEN

THERE was a breakfast room leading off the kitchen in the Beltrees homestead. It overlooked the lake and, unlike the rather grand decor of the rest of the house, was country cottagey with a pine dresser laden with blue and white crockery. There was a hatstand laden with Akubras and other hats and a rack for coats, as well as baskets, and on a side-table lay the odds and ends of a riding family: whips, bits and the like.

Aurora was sitting at the breakfast table contemplating bacon, a poached egg and a fried tomato. It was a chilly, overcast day with the lake reflecting the leaden sky above. The swans, which she had seen engaging in a love dance that had made her think of the ballet, *Swan Lake*, were tucked into the reeds on the far bank.

She wore a forest-green pullover with navy track-suit trousers and her hair was tied back severely. Her green eyes mirrored the chaotic emotions that had claimed her since Luke had reacted so savagely to *her* uncertain reaction on the subject of marrying him.

For a moment she'd wondered whether she might break when his arms had tightened around her like a steel trap. Then he'd sworn ferociously and, if you could slam out of a bed, that was what he'd done, leaving her entirely to her own devices.

She'd tried to think about it for some time, then got up and had a shower and dressed. She'd found him in the break-fast room, also showered, from the damp look of his hair, shaved and dressed in jeans and a navy sweater. But the look he'd cast her as she'd come in had been so damning

169

and dangerous, she'd paused in the doorway and contemplated flight.

Causing him to say caustically that he wasn't going to eat *her*, but breakfast was served.

Now, she picked up her knife and fork and started on her meal.

'Would you care to enlarge on your earlier statement, Aurora?' he drawled as he pushed his plate away and reached for the marmalade.

'If you didn't know what was on the cards, why did you come here with me? I did tell you, though. Coffee?'

'Yes, thank you. Uh...' She looked pointedly at the open door leading to the kitchen where she could hear the housekeeper, a voluble, friendly matron, clattering about. 'I don't think this is the right time or place—'

'There's never going to be a better time,' he interrupted, but got up to close the door, not gently.

Aurora grimaced. 'You actually said you were contemplating asking me to marry you, Luke, but in the four days since then you haven't mentioned it again. All right...' she shrugged '...semantics, perhaps, but—why did I come? I couldn't help myself.' She returned his gaze directly. 'That doesn't mean to say marriage is the answer for us.'

'If you're about to cite Leonie, I have it on good authority that she has a new man in her life,' he said coolly. 'If you're about to cite how you came into my life virtually on her heels, we've now known each for something like five months, the last two of which we've spent apart. Time, don't you think,' he said sardonically, 'for me to have sorted myself out?'

Aurora finished her bacon and eggs and reached for her coffee-cup. 'And yet, Luke,' she said steadily, 'if my father hadn't got himself lost, we would still be apart. You've put the house on the market—'

'How did you know that? It hasn't been advertised.'

'Remember Mrs Bunnings? She used to be our housekeeper and Miss Hillier employed her as a cleaner—until a month or so ago when she went to Adelaide to look after her sick sister. We keep in touch.'

He digested this, all the while allowing that dark, arrogant gaze to play over her. 'All right, let's take another tack. Do you usually sleep with men in the uninhibited way you sleep with me, then walk out on them? Or—are you offering to be my mistress?'

Aurora took an unsteady breath and a glint of anger lit her eyes. 'I'm offering you nothing at the moment, Luke. This all happened because I was under extreme pressure one way or another, and because you came to my rescue when I never felt more alone or bereft in my life. I—'

'Only because of your father, Aurora? Or because you were missing me as well?'

She swallowed some coffee, then tilted her chin at him. 'Both. That's my problem, however. But I walked away from you once, Luke, when I wasn't sure you wanted a wife, when I was *quite* sure things weren't over between you and Leonie—and I'm quite capable of doing it again.'

'I haven't seen Leonie from that day to this,' he said.

Her eyes widened.

He smiled satanically. 'What exactly do I have to do to prove to you I want not only a wife but *you*?' he asked lethally. 'Who took whom to the moon last night, incidentally?' His eyes were suddenly mocking.

Her hands trembled around her coffee-cup.

'Don't you think that proves anything?' He eyed her satirically. 'I rather thought it proved something to you when you woke up this morning looking, anyway, so gloriously serene. You could almost say the joke was on me.'

'It's still no reason to rush to the altar, Luke,' she said barely audibly.

'How long would you like, then? A couple of months? Three? That might be a bit hard to arrange because I'm moving up here for the next three months, but I guess we could commute.'

Aurora stood up carefully and for a moment, before she blinked, tears glittered in her eyes. They were gone, however, when she said crisply, 'I'd like to go home today, please. Because I'm now quite sure we wouldn't suit, Luke.'

His mouth was hard. 'I hesitate to repeat your often-spoken phrase, Aurora, but is that all you've got to say?'

'No, it isn't. You should never confuse lust with love, Luke. I would have thought, to be honest, you wouldn't need that explained to you.'

'Lust?' he said softly and incredulously.

She clenched her hands. 'As well as friendship, of course—I'll always be grateful for the way you came to me that night. But since there's no way I can prove to *myself* it wasn't a bit of both for a girl who also tugged a chord of pity in you, I think we should leave it there.'

'Lust,' he said again, and this time there was so much sardonic irony in his eyes, she flinched. But he stood up too and came round the table to be directly in front of her, so she was literally being towered over. 'If that's how it came across, Aurora, if that's what you feel you yourself were indulging in…' he paused and waited while her eyes flickered beneath the insult, then went on '…I think you should go home this morning. The plane is going down to Brisbane to pick Dad up, leaving in half an hour. Would that suit you?'

He'd spoken quite mildly but Aurora knew she was on the receiving end of the full force of Luke Kirwan at his most bored and dismissive.

'It would suit me fine,' she whispered, so hurt but also so angry, she was amazed she could speak at all. 'Please don't wait around to see me off. I'm sure someone could run me to the airstrip.'

'Why not,' he murmured, 'if that's what you want?'

'It is.'

He smiled, taking in the strained lines of her face, the sudden pallor, but the fire in her eyes. 'Well, goodbye, Aurora. You've been a few things to me, a cat burglar, a pocket señorita, an unusual lover, a girl who could never resist a challenge—until it came to this. Or perhaps you meant it when you said you intended to stay into "fun" for a good while to come?'

She refused to speak.

He drew the outline of her face with his fingers, then formed a fist to rest it beneath her chin. 'Stay safe, little one.' And he turned away to stroll out of the room.

Aurora was able to hold onto her anger as a means of keeping her composure until she got home. Then it fled away from her as she stared at her goldfish—her neighbour had fed them while she'd been away—and it came home to her that, even while she hated Luke Kirwan, her life seemed to stretch before her in a succession of long, lonely days with only two fish to confide in...

How could he not have understood that, if nothing else, she needed time to think? He was the one who had stepped back from marriage at almost the last moment. He was the one who got these 'calls' to go off and do his own thing, and hadn't been able to see how a wife could understand without feeling slighted. He was the one who *had* accepted her reasoning the last time and rearranged his life accordingly—until her father had got himself lost.

She dumped her bag down at her feet and went to make herself a cup of tea. It was no nicer a day on the coast than up beyond Charleville. Grey, cold and miserable, which was exactly how she felt, she mused as she curled up on the settee with her cup in her hands.

But why did she also feel as if she'd done something wrong?

The thought came to her from nowhere and the word 'lust'

followed straight on its heels. She swallowed a mouthful of tea. She hadn't really meant that, she reflected. It had been a jibe uttered out of anger as well as despair because he had not even attempted to understand how she felt. Yet it had never felt like lust between them…

It had been too wonderful to describe in that term, but she had, and had it turned lethally back on her. Deservedly? Perhaps. Did it make much difference though? she asked herself sadly. Did it alter her conviction that circumstance and pity, rather than real love, had caused Luke to offer her marriage? Or, even if it was real love, could it survive between them?

She finished her tea and contemplated the fact that she had three more days before she started work—and had it to sustain her. And knew suddenly that she couldn't bear three days home alone brooding, she couldn't bear the thought of going to bed alone upstairs because the last time she'd slept in her bed had been the first time she'd slept with Luke Kirwan.

It was so strange, she thought. Once she'd got to know him that arrogant, damningly bored man had become someone quite different, someone she adored—she couldn't deny it as, at last, the tears began to fall. But that dangerous side had come back and she'd run headlong into it.

She put her cup down, wiped her streaming eyes with her fingers and came to a sudden decision. Ten minutes later, after having asked her neighbour to feed the fish again, she was in her car driving north to the Sunshine Coast, hoping to find some sun and solace for the next three days.

'Welcome back! You're looking well, Aurora,' Neil said the next Monday morning. 'All set and rarin' to go? Did you have fun with your father?'

'Thanks, thanks, yes and yes in that order, Neil,' she replied jauntily. 'But I didn't persuade him to come home.'

Neil grimaced. 'Let's hope he's got all the bad luck behind him, then. You have been missed, Miss Templeton! Lots of calls bemoaning the lack of your golden voice on the airwaves.'

'That's...gratifying!'

'There is another piece of news I thought might be of interest to you.' Neil watched her thoughtfully for a moment.

Aurora raised an eyebrow at him.

'Leonie Murdoch has got herself engaged. When she began to be seen in the company of a new man we all thought she was giving Luke the old sauce for the gander, sauce for the goose routine. But Mandy reckons she's really fallen for this bloke.'

'Good,' Aurora said slowly.

'You don't sound too sure,' Neil commented.

Aurora had been staring unseeingly at the console. She shrugged. 'It's none of my business.'

Neil stared at her penetratingly, opened his mouth, then apparently decided against commenting. 'How would you like to interview the Leader of the State Opposition?'

Aurora blinked. 'As in talking politics?'

Neil shook his head. 'As in discussing her pet hobby—growing native Australian bush tucker. Which is not to say the coverage won't provide some political coverage for her, but all you have to be is strictly neutral. When I say "all", it's a bit of a challenge, actually,' he added, casting Aurora a fleeting glance. 'If you were to have any strong political leanings one way or the other, for example.'

But Aurora intercepted that fleeting glance and got the uncomfortable feeling that Neil had seen through her carefully erected defences on the subject of Luke Kirwan, and was offering this as bait to help her over it.

Which was just what she needed, she reminded herself. 'OK! How long have I got to prepare for it?'

'That's my girl,' Neil said quietly. 'Three days.'

Two weeks later, on her way home from work, Aurora saw a yellow Saab turn the corner ahead of her, the corner that led up the hill to her old home.

Perhaps Luke was back for a quick visit before the house was sold, she told herself. Or perhaps it was one of any number of yellow Saabs there might be around. But they were not that common, she knew…

That same night she got a phone call from Bunny, back from visiting her sister in Adelaide and full of the news that she'd got her old job back.

'The dragon lady told me the woman they hired to replace me was a disaster and there've been two more since,' she said triumphantly down the line. 'Mind you, you have to be something special to put up with her, but I can't help feeling as pleased as punch.'

'That's great, Bunny,' Aurora said slowly, 'but I thought the house was up for sale?'

'It was for a while but the professor has changed his mind, it seems. And he's spending a lot more time at home these days. Actually, he's a lovely man, not at all what I first thought he was, but then I didn't get to meet him for ages, did I?'

'I…I thought he was spending three months or… thereabouts out west on the family sheep station,' Aurora said raggedly.

'Miss Hillier reckons he's had a change of plan, but how's my little girl going?' Bunny asked breezily.

Aurora stared at the phone for ages after she put it down.

Then she wrapped her arms around her and closed her eyes. What did it mean? What did this tense, jumpy feeling that had invaded her mean for her? That she hadn't given up hope?

She couldn't sleep that night and was incredibly restless for the next couple of days, but nothing happened. No yellow Saab pulling up in front of her house, no phone call, no nothing. And she couldn't believe the pain it caused her to put her hopes to rest once again. Her life reminded her of the autumn equinox: short, desperately busy days, long cold nights and the chill feeling it would be like this for the rest of her life…

Then she got a cold, lost her voice, and had to take a few days off work. At the same time Neil decided to cut her workload so she could concentrate on her music and talk-back programmes. She was in two minds about it—not having to get up at five-thirty in the morning to read the news would be a relief in normal circumstances, but pushing herself to the limits in these circumstances seemed to be about the only way she could cope with life without Luke.

It was a Friday and she was due back at work on Monday, when a lovely basket of fruit and flowers was delivered.

She answered the door and the delivery man said cheerfully, 'Mrs Newton? These are for you.'

'I think you've got the wrong address, I'm not Mrs Newton—' She stopped abruptly.

The man scratched his head and consulted his clipboard. 'Nope, this is the address I've got here.'

'Is there a message?'

They inspected the basket together but there was nothing. 'OK, I'll check back with the shop,' the delivery man said, and pulled out his mobile phone.

Two minutes later he switched it off and pushed it into his pocket. 'The address is right and it was ordered by a man who came in and paid cash for it but he didn't want to send a message—said you'd know what it was all about. He did give his name, though—Isaac Newton.' It was his turn to stop abruptly and look at her acutely. 'Got to be some kind of a joke, right? Even if they didn't twig at the shop, I'm pretty damn sure Isaac Newton isn't wandering round Manly!' He laughed.

'No. Yes. Um…I mean, thanks. I think I know who must have sent them.'

*   *   *

She set the basket on her elephant coffee-table, sat down on the settee and stared at it with her chin in her hands for ages. It had to be a peace-offering—or did it? Perhaps Luke had simply heard via Neil that she was off sick? But...Mrs Newton?

She nearly jumped out of her skin when the phone rang. And she dropped the remote and seemed to be all fingers and thumbs before she got it to her ear.

'Hello...'

'Mrs Newton? This is Carla from the Sheraton Mirage on the Gold Coast. How are you?'

'I...I'm not...I'm...fine,' Aurora said dazedly.

'Mrs Newton, Mr Newton presents his compliments and we have a room reserved for you for tonight and instructions to book a limo to pick you up, should you feel like taking this reservation up—Mr Newton asked me to tell you it was entirely up to you. But, if so, we wondered what time you'd like to be collected?'

Aurora's mouth fell open.

'Ma'am?' Carla of the Sheraton Mirage prompted discreetly after the silence had stretched. 'I believe you're in Brisbane—Manly, actually. It would take about an hour to get down here,' she added helpfully.

Aurora tried to collect herself and looked at her watch. It was two o'clock in the afternoon but... 'Around four?' she heard herself say tentatively. 'Would that...?' She couldn't go on.

'I'll arrange for the limo to be at your door at four, Mrs Newton, and may I say that we look forward to welcoming you to the Mirage!'

'What have I done?' Aurora said to the phone as it went dead in her hands. 'What does this *mean*?' She jumped up agitatedly. More pressure to marry him—but why? Surely she'd let him off the hook... And why wasn't he at Beltrees seeking meteorite fragments?

*   *   *

She was still in a state of shock and confusion when the limousine drew up outside the Sheraton Mirage. Then it dawned on her she was going to have to masquerade as 'Mrs Newton' unless Luke was there to meet her, but as she got out of the car and looked around anxiously there was no sign of him.

But as she stood poised, as if for flight, a staff member with a name tag pinned to her jacket bustled forward. It was Carla and she greeted Aurora profusely and offered to lead her to her room. All the check-in formalities had been completed, she confided as they walked through the foyer.

'Is...is Mr Newton around?' Aurora asked hesitantly.

'I'm sure he will be, ma'am,' Carla said serenely.

An hour later there was no sign of Luke so Aurora decided to go for a walk.

It was a wild, overcast day with a strong breeze whipping up the surf and the odd squall passing through. Aurora wore a fleecy-lined track suit and a yellow raincoat as she battled up the beach, head down in the teeth of a minor gale, and battled with the unreality of things.

What was going on? Why had he invited her down, then not even been there to meet her? Was she in the middle of some kind of dream?

She stopped at last, breathless and worried about her voice—it was the last thing she should be doing, braving the elements on top of a recent cold, but she hadn't stopped to think. She *couldn't* think.

She turned around and at least the wind was behind her—then she saw him. A lone, tall figure quite a way from her, but there was no mistaking Luke Kirwan—at least, not for her.

It was a spontaneous reaction, what happened next. She started to run towards him, stumbling in the sand, and he quickened his pace. And she ran right into his arms, crying with frustration and despair...

'Why are you doing this, Luke? I don't know what's going on, I don't know what to think, I don't know why I came—I'm a mess!' she wept.

His arms closed around her. 'Aurora.' He held her closer than he ever had. 'I'm sorry! But I couldn't convince myself you'd really come.'

'I'm sorry,' he said again, this time in the warmth of her room with the shutters closed against the wild weather and lamps on giving the room a gentle glow.

He'd insisted she change into dry clothes and poured them each a brandy. He'd insisted she dry her hair properly and asked her several times if she was warm enough.

Now, as she sat on the settee with her legs curled up beneath her, with no more to be done but feel the warmth of the brandy slip through her veins, he stood in front of her, looking down at her sombrely. Nothing, in the bustle of getting her back to the room, dry and changed, had transpired between them to explain anything, although the way he'd held her in that moment on the beach had given her a slender, delicate little ray of hope. But it flickered beneath this sombre regard and a sense of dread began to take its place.

'Luke,' she said as the words built up in her head and wouldn't be denied, 'I've tried so hard to forget you and convince myself I was right, but it's not working. I know you don't really want a wife but I couldn't be worse off than I am without you, so—'

She stopped as a shudder ran through his tall frame and he sat down in front of her on a padded stool. His hair was still damp and hanging in his eyes. The hollows beneath his cheekbones that she'd always found so fascinating were more pronounced and he looked as if he'd lost weight beneath his navy jumper and bone cord trousers.

'Aurora,' he said with quiet intensity, 'in the space of

getting to know you, I've gone from not really wanting a wife to knowing that I shan't rest until I get one—you.'

She gasped, her green eyes huge.

'I feel like a ship without a rudder. I can't settle to anything, I've lost all interest in meteorites, I couldn't care less how it may have worked for Galileo, living without *you*— is not going to work for me.'

'Luke...'

But he held up a hand. 'This is not something I'm proud of, but I can only say I didn't understand. What love really was, I mean. Yes, Leonie was my companion and my bedmate for three years, but it never filled me with a kind of terror to wake up in the night and think I might have lost her for good. That's what it does to me to think I've lost you. That's why you'd be no good as my mistress, Aurora, if that's what you were going to say—I should spend my life petrified I was going to lose you. I'm sorry, but that's how it is.'

'So it really has nothing to do with...a girl with only two goldfish and a diary to confide in?' she asked tremulously.

'None whatsoever—it's the opposite, if anything. I don't even have a diary or some fish to sustain me. The first time you walked away from me...' he paused and closed his eyes briefly '...I told myself you were better off without a man like me. At the same time, though, I asked myself why I felt as if I was letting something more precious than ruby and pearls slip through my fingers.'

Her lips parted in soundless incredulity.

He smiled, but it was strained. 'The second time you walked away from me I was being entirely unreasonable and I damn well knew it, but I couldn't help myself because I just didn't know how to get through to you.' He shrugged. 'My male ego took an awful hammering that morning.'

Two tears slid down Aurora's cheeks and she sniffed.

He pulled a large blue hanky from his pocket and handed it to her.

She wiped her nose.

'Please,' he said softly, 'don't tell me you still believe it was lust between us. I couldn't stand it. I love everything about you, Aurora. I'm lost without you. I need you more than you may ever know.'

She stared at him wordlessly and read the unflinching honesty in his eyes. Then she put her glass down and leant forward to cup his face in her hands. 'Mr Newton,' she said huskily, 'I need *you* more than I ever dreamt I'd need any-one.'

'You've done it again,' he said, in a teasing paraphrase of what she'd once said to him.

She stirred drowsily in his arms. The night was dark out-side and it was still blowing a minor gale, but beneath the covers of her bed they were naked and sated after a glorious lovemaking. 'Tell me.'

'You've bestowed that sheer joyful spirit like a beautiful butterfly in the guise of a gorgeous girl on me, Aurora. I love you.'

She snuggled against him, revelling in the planes and an-gles of his body and how soft and silky she felt against him, how he'd transported her to the moon again, although this time they'd gone together and matched each other every step of the way.

'Mind you...' he stroked her back, then buried his head briefly in her hair '...I can't help having qualms about re-peating myself. Will you marry me, Aurora? There, it's out,' he said humorously, looking into her eyes.

'Luke, I would love to marry you,' she said. 'It's quite simple, really—I adore you.'

'Aurora—' He stopped, then went on, 'Is that really true?'

'Oh, yes,' she assured him, and he could see it in her eyes in a way that took his breath away. He buried his head be-tween her breasts and she stroked his hair.

Then he looked up reluctantly. 'Even...the absent-minded

professor in me, the guy who gets strange calls to do strange things and all the rest?' There was a question mark in his dark eyes.

'Well, there may be times when I'll blame the apple too,' she said gravely, 'but—what we feel for each other will find a way, don't you think?'

'I always knew you were wise as well as gorgeous,' he said a little unsteadily.

'Actually, you started off thinking I was a groupie, Professor,' she reminded him.

'I learnt that lesson the hard way,' he said wryly. 'But there are several things you didn't take into consideration about me. What good husband material I would make, how romantic I could be—'

'Luke—' she started to laugh, then kissed him back '—you're right, I certainly didn't expect…this.' She gestured with a wondering expression on her face, to take it all in: the hotel, the limo, the plans he'd made, Mrs Newton…

'And you haven't seen this yet.' He sat up and reached for his trousers flung across the bottom of the bed.

Aurora traced the long line of his back and felt the muscles flow beneath the skin. 'This' was a black velvet box drawn from the pocket of his trousers. She sat up, brushing her hair back, and stared at it.

'Open it,' he said quietly, putting it into her hand.

She flicked the lid up and went absolutely still. It was a pearl engagement ring exquisitely set in a circlet of tiny rubies and diamonds.

'You…meant it,' she whispered at last, looking up into his dark eyes.

'Every last word of it, Aurora. I hope that every time you look at it, you'll know just how much you do mean to me.'

'Luke…' she rested her head on his shoulder and her voice shook '…thank you, but I've got nothing for you in return.'

'Darling—' he took her in his arms and kissed her lingeringly '—every time you feel like singing when we make love is a priceless gift for me.'

Her lips quivered. 'I knew you'd never let me forget that—' She stopped suddenly. 'Actually, I do have something for you—where did I put my bag? Oh, there it is.'

It was on the bedside table. She opened it and drew out a tiny suede drawstring bag. She undid the ties and poured the contents into the palm of her hand—a very fine gold chain with a milky-blue opal mounted in gold and hanging from it. 'Do you remember this?'

He nodded, staring down at the opal.

'I got it set and put on the chain and, right up until this afternoon, I've worn it next to my heart—I felt if I couldn't have you, I could have this little part of you as a good luck charm and something to remind me of the only man in the world I wanted to love.'

He took it from her and put it over her head, and he settled the stone between her breasts. Then he held her very close. 'Thanks,' he said unevenly into her hair. 'I don't know what to say.'

'Don't say anything,' she suggested, and she slipped her arms round his neck and started to croon against the corner of his mouth, an old song... 'Fly me to the moon...' She broke off and there were tears of joy in her eyes, although she said whimsically, 'How appropriate is that, Professor?'

He lay back with her and murmured wryly, 'Singularly appropriate and—request granted, ma'am.' He did just that.

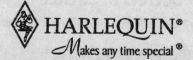

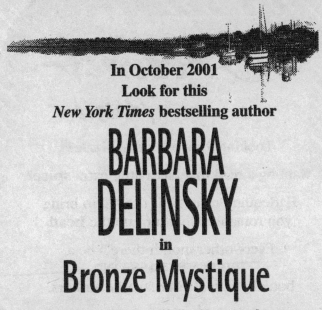

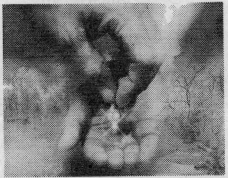
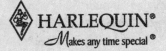

Harlequin Romance®
Love affairs that
last a lifetime.

HARLEQUIN *Presents~*
Seduction and passion
guaranteed.

Harlequin® Historical®
Historical
Romantic
Adventure.

HARLEQUIN®
Temptation.
Sassy, sexy, seductive!

HARLEQUIN *Super* ROMANCE®
Emotional,
exciting,
unexpected.

HARLEQUIN® *American Romance®*
Heart, home
& happiness.

HARLEQUIN®
Duets™
Romantic comedy.

HARLEQUIN®
INTRIGUE®
Breathtaking
romantic suspense.

HARLEQUIN® *Blaze™*
Red-Hot Reads.

HARLEQUIN®
Makes any time special®